YORK NOTES

General Editors: Professor A.N. Jeffares (*University of Stirling*) & Professor Suheil Bushrui (*American University of Beirut*)

Jane Austen

PERSUASION

Notes by Angela Smith

MA (BIRMINGHAM) M LITT (CAMBRIDGE)
Lecturer in English Studies, University of Stirling

**LONGMAN
YORK PRESS**

YORK PRESS
Immeuble Esseily, Place Riad Solh, Beirut.

LONGMAN GROUP UK LIMITED
Longman House, Burnt Mill, Harlow,
Essex CM20 2JE, England
Associated companies, branches and representatives
throughout the world

First published 1980
Sixth impression 1991

ISBN 0-582-03578-3

Produced by Longman Group (FE) Ltd.
Printed in Hong Kong

Contents

Part 1

Introduction

The life of Jane Austen

At the time that Jane Austen was writing *Persuasion* she wrote to one of her nieces about another who had become pregnant again immediately after the birth of a second daughter:

> Anna has not a chance of escape . . . Poor Animal, she will be worn out before she is thirty. I am very sorry for her. Mrs Clement too is in that way again. I am quite tired of so many Children. Mrs Benn has a 13th.*

There is a harshness about the phrase 'poor animal' suggestive of strong feeling; it sounds bitterly reductive but we realise that the tone is disappointed rather than contemptuous when the description of Anna written a month earlier in a letter is compared with it:

> She looked so pretty, it was quite a pleasure to see her, so young and so blooming and so innocent, as if she had never had a wicked Thought in her Life.†

Such letters as these bely the impression which the *Memoir*‡ tends to create that Jane Austen lived a life of cosy domesticity. Certainly she was part of an affectionate close-knit family, although painful facts are glossed over in the *Memoir*; there is no mention of her second brother, George, who lived to be seventy-two but was defective in some way. She was born at Steventon, in Hampshire, on 16 December 1775, the year in which James Watt invented the steam-engine; her father was a clergyman and she had six brothers and a sister. Her father, who had been known as 'the handsome proctor' when he was at Oxford, was an intelligent man who encouraged his children to read widely; her mother was the niece of a Master of Balliol College, Oxford, who was renowned for his wit.

Though her father taught his sons at home, Jane Austen and her elder sister, Cassandra, were sent to school briefly; her formal schooling finished by the time she was about ten, and from then on she remained

---

*Letters, edited by R.W. Chapman, Oxford University Press, London, 1952, Letter of 23 March 1817, p.488

†*Letters*, 20 February 1817, p.481

‡J.E. Austen-Leigh, *A Memoir of Jane Austen* (1871); republished in Jane Austen, *Persuasion*, ed. D.W. Harding, Penguin Books, Harmondsworth, 1965

at home. She seems to have begun writing when she was very young, dedicating her stories to members of her family. Most of her juvenilia are parodies, often of the sentimental novels fashionable when she was young; the heroine of *Northanger Abbey*, Catherine Morland, is an avid reader of this kind of fiction. When she was fourteen, Jane Austen wrote *Love and Freindship* (her spelling is erratic in the letters she wrote as an adult), which is a story told in letters, as popular novels of the time often were. The typical heroine had a classical name, was beautiful, and so sensitive that she might rave hysterically. Jane Austen's Laura is such a one:

> 'Talk not to me of Phaetons (said I, raving in a frantic, incoherent manner)—Give me a violin—. I'll play to him and sooth him in his melancholy Hours—Beware ye gentle Nymphs of Cupid's Thunderbolts, avoid the piercing shafts of Jupiter—Look at that grove of Firs —I see a Leg of Mutton—They told me Edward was not Dead; but they deceived me—they took him for a cucumber—' Thus I continued wildly exclaiming on my Edward's Death . . . She was a Widow and had only one Daughter, who was then just seventeen— One of the best of ages; but alas! she was very plain and her name was Bridget . . . Nothing therfore could be expected from her—she could not be supposed to possess either exalted Ideas, Delicate Feelings or refined Sensibilities—. She was nothing more than a mere good-tempered, civil and obliging young woman; as such we could scarcely dislike her—she was only an Object of Contempt—.*

In *The History of England*, dedicated to her sister and written when she was fifteen, Jane Austen makes clear that she is not an impartial historian:

> *Henry the 6th*
> I cannot say much for this Monarch's sense. Nor would I if I could, for he was a Lancastrian. I suppose you know all about the Wars between him and the Duke of York who was of the right side; if you do not, you had better read some other History, for I shall not be very diffuse in this, meaning by it only to vent my spleen *against*, and shew my Hatred *to* all those people whose parties or principles do not suit with mine, and not to give information.†

When she was older she advised nephews and nieces who were trying to write novels to read as much as they could and leave writing till later; she refers to herself as 'the most unlearned and uninformed female who ever dared to be an authoress'‡ and seems to regret the time she spent on early writing.

***Love and Freindship*, Chatto and Windus, London, 1929. Letter the 13th, p.32
†*Love and Freindship*, The History of England: Henry the 6th, p.86
‡*Letters*, 11 December 1815, p.443

Her brothers mostly had distinguished careers; James was a clergyman, and Francis and Charles both became admirals. Edward was the adopted heir of a rich country gentleman, like Frank Churchill in Jane Austen's novel *Emma* (1816) whose estate he inherited. Henry, Jane's adviser on publishing and business matters, had a chequered career: from Oxford he went into the Oxford Militia, then into banking in London. He was declared bankrupt in 1816, three years after the death of his first wife, and then took holy orders and was a country clergyman for the rest of his life. Cassandra Austen was engaged to a young clergyman who died in the West Indies in 1797 where he was chaplain to a regiment; she never married and remained at home.

While she lived in the rectory at Steventon Jane Austen wrote the first versions of *Sense and Sensibility* (1811), *Pride and Prejudice* (1813) and *Northanger Abbey* (1818). She seems always to have given social and domestic duties priority over her writing; her nephew describes how she worked when he knew her:

> She had no separate study to retire to, and most of the work must have been done in the general sitting-room, subject to all kinds of casual interruptions. She was careful that her occupation should not be suspected by servants, or visitors, or any persons beyond her own family party. She wrote upon small sheets of paper which could easily be put away, or covered with a piece of blotting paper. There was, between the front door and the offices, a swing door which creaked when it was opened; but she objected to having this little inconvenience remedied, because it gave her notice when anyone was coming.*

She lived an ordinary life for a young woman of her class; her letters describe balls and new clothes, and she obviously had admirers. She was attractive and lively:

> In person she was very attractive; her figure was rather tall and slender, her step light and firm, and her whole appearance expressive of health and animation. In complexion she was a clear brunette with a rich colour; she had full round cheeks, with mouth and nose small and well formed, bright hazel eyes, and brown hair forming natural curls close round her face. If not so regularly handsome as her sister, yet her countenance had a peculiar charm of its own to the eyes of most beholders.†

When she was twenty-five her father retired and moved the family home to Bath, to Jane Austen's great regret, as she disliked towns. At about this time (1801) she seems to have fallen in love, while she was on holi-

Memoir, ch.5, pp.339–40
†*Memoir*, ch.5, p.330

day at the seaside. Her sister Cassandra destroyed all her intimate letters after Jane Austen's death, so little is known of this incident. The man she loved was to have visited her at home but died before he could do so. In 1802 she accepted an offer of marriage but then immediately withdrew the acceptance, and afterwards settled into a premature middle age:

> I believe that she and her sister were generally thought to have taken to the garb of middle age earlier than their years or their looks required; and that, though remarkably neat in their dress as in all their ways, they were scarcely sufficiently regardful of the fashionable, or the becoming.‡

While the family were in Bath Mr Austen died suddenly; Mrs Austen and her daughters moved first to Southampton and then to Chawton in Hampshire, to a cottage in the grounds of Edward's house. Here Jane Austen revised and published *Sense and Sensibility* in 1811, anonymously at her own expense. *Pride and Prejudice* was published in 1813; she refers to it in a letter to Cassandra as 'my own darling child' and to Elizabeth Bennet as being 'as delightful a creature as ever appeared in print, and how I shall be able to tolerate those who do not like *her* at least I do not know'.* *Northanger Abbey* had been sold to a publisher in Bath for £10 in 1803 but was never published by him. Her brother Henry retrieved the manuscript and copyright from him; meanwhile *Mansfield Park* was finished and published in 1814, and *Emma* in 1815.

Though she made less than £700 from her novels they had some distinguished admirers, including Sir Walter Scott and the Prince Regent, who kept a set of her novels at each of his houses and to whom *Emma* is dedicated. She seems to have disliked the idea of becoming a literary figure, and remained at Chawton, becoming increasingly ill with what has subsequently been diagnosed as Addison's Disease. Cassandra nursed her and moved her to Winchester in the hope of finding better medical treatment, but Jane Austen died there on 18 July 1817, and was buried in the Cathedral. As she was dying she said, 'God grant me patience, Pray for me oh Pray for me'.† *Persuasion* and *Northanger Abbey* were published together posthumously with a biographical notice written by her brother in December 1817.

Jane Austen in her time

There are certain events in Jane Austen's life which remind us that, secluded as she was, she was nevertheless as much a part of the external

‡*Memoir*, ch.5, p.330
Letters, 29 January 1813, p.297
†*Letters*, Appendix, p.514

world as we are. Her cousin, Eliza, whose parents were friends of
Warren Hastings in India, was educated in Paris and married the Comte
de Feuillide. During the French Revolution in 1794 the Comte was
guillotined; his wife, an elegant and sophisticated woman, escaped to
England. She stayed at Steventon; Jane Austen seems to have admired
her, and had dedicated *Love and Freindship* to her in 1790. Eliza married
Jane Austen's brother Henry in 1797 and together they went to France
during the Peace of Amiens to try to recover some of the Comte's
property. Napoleon had ordered that all English travellers should be
detained but Eliza's French was so perfect that their nationality was
not discovered and they escaped.

The Napoleonic Wars lasted until 1815, with only the brief Peace of
Amiens in 1802. This must have caused the Austen family worry as two
of the Austen brothers were in the navy; the end of *Persuasion* suggests
the nagging anxiety felt by women whose loved ones might have to
fight at sea. There are recurrent references throughout Jane Austen's
letters to the whereabouts of her naval brothers.

There were hazards, apart from those involved in childbirth, to be
met with at home also. Two of Jane Austen's close friends were killed
in accidents with horses, and her aunt was charged with theft from a
shop. This seems a relatively insignificant event, but in 1800 the penalty
for theft was death or transportation. She was in custody for eight
months; it seems she was charged in the hope that she could be black-
mailed since she was a wealthy woman. She was eventually acquitted
but the experience must have brought her family into close contact
with some of the more brutal aspects of their society.

There is a callousness about using the death sentence as a penalty for
a minor theft that was perhaps part of the moral atmosphere in which
Jane Austen lived; occasionally she displays a harshness which sits ill
with what her relations say about her. Her nephew claims that in life
she 'never played with its serious duties or responsibilities, nor did she
ever turn individuals into ridicule'.‡ Perhaps the writer had not seen
the letter about Mrs Hall of Sherbourne who 'was brought to bed
yesterday of a dead child, some weeks before she expected, owing to a
fright. I suppose she happened unawares to look at her husband.'* This
was written to her sister when she was very young and may have a
private significance; it was not, of course, intended for publication.
However, the same tone is to be found, infrequently, in the novels, as in
the description of fat Mrs Musgrove's grief for her dead son in
Persuasion :

Personal size and mental sorrow have certainly no necessary proportions. A large bulky figure has as good a right to be in deep affliction,

‡ *Memoir*, ch.5, p.333
* *Letters*, 27 October 1798, p.24

as the most graceful set of limbs in the world. But, fair or not fair, there are unbecoming conjunctions, which reason will patronize in vain,—which taste cannot tolerate,—which ridicule will seize. (Chapter 8)

The detached coldness of this insistence on good taste seems worthy of Sir Walter Elliot rather than of the narrator who mostly endorses the view of the sensitive and humane heroine. It represents a tension that must have been a part of Jane Austen's intellectual and artistic experience. She was a contemporary of all the great English Romantics, and of Scott, and she quotes from Byron and Scott, yet she also admired the great Augustans: she refers in her letters to 'my dear Dr Johnson'† and claims of the poet that there 'has been one infallible Pope in the world'.‡ Augustan good sense meets a belief in what the romantic poet John Keats (1795–1821) called 'the holiness of the Heart's affections'* in Jane Austen's novels.

A note on the text

Persuasion was first published after Jane Austen's death, together with *Northanger Abbey*, early in 1818. It was prefaced by an introductory note written by her brother Henry, giving a brief account of her life. As a result of the fact that the novel was published posthumously the author could not check the proofs, and there are a few textual problems. In the original edition the novel was divided into two volumes, the first ending at the conclusion of Chapter 12. Modern editions mostly number the chapters continuously. The cancelled chapter was first printed in the second edition of J.E. Austen-Leigh's *Memoir*, in 1871.

The definitive edition of *Persuasion* is contained in Vol. V of *The Novels of Jane Austen*, edited by R.W. Chapman, Clarendon Press, Oxford, 1923; in it he collated early editions and supplied very full notes.

†*Letters*, 8 February 1807, p.181
‡*Letters*, 26 October 1813, p.362
The Letters of John Keats, edited by Maurice Buxton Forman, Fourth edition, Oxford University Press, London, 1952. Letter 31, 22 November 1817, p.67

Part 2

Summaries
of PERSUASION

A general summary

Sir Walter Elliot, the widower father of three grown-up daughters, is in financial difficulties and is persuaded by his agent Mr Shepherd to rent his home, Kellynch Hall, to a tenant and to move to Bath. His friend Lady Russell approves of this idea as she wishes Sir Walter's second daughter, Anne, to mix in society more, and she hopes that the move will put an end to an unsuitable friendship which Elizabeth, Sir Walter's eldest daughter, has formed with Mrs Clay. Mrs Clay is Mr Shepherd's daughter who has returned to live with him after an unhappy marriage; she flatters Elizabeth and Sir Walter who seem to prefer her company to Anne's.

Admiral Croft, a married but childless man, is accepted as a tenant for Kellynch Hall, a fact which disturbs Anne. Seven years earlier his brother-in-law, Captain Frederick Wentworth, a naval officer, had been engaged to marry Anne, but her father and Lady Russell disapproved of the engagement so strongly that it was broken off. Captain Wentworth resented Anne's treatment of him and she never met anyone who could take his place, though she received a proposal from Charles Musgrove who subsequently married her younger sister, Mary. Anne has read in the newspapers that Captain Wentworth has risen in his profession.

Anne goes to stay with Mary at Uppercross when her father and sister move to Bath where she helps the discontented Mary to look after her two children and visits Charles Musgrove's parents in the Great House. They are friendly hospitable people with a large family including two pretty grown-up daughters, Henrietta and Louisa. The Crofts move into Kellynch and Captain Wentworth comes to stay with them, and calls at Uppercross. He meets Anne and she hears that he thinks her so changed that he would not have known her; she knows her youthful prettiness has faded as a result of her separation from the man she loves. Captain Wentworth has never met anyone like Anne but still resents her treatment of him and wants to marry any eligible woman but her.

Captain Wentworth stays on at Kellynch, causing mixed feelings in the families at Uppercross. Louisa and Henrietta seem infatuated with him, which annoys Charles Hayter, the Musgroves' cousin, a young curate generally expected to marry Henrietta. Anne is embarrassed by finding herself alone with them one day in Mary's house; her two-year-old nephew climbs on her back and she cannot get him off until Captain Wentworth gently releases her. She is moved by this incident, and by other small indications that he still has some interest in her and notices when she is tired. Charles Hayter and Henrietta are reconciled and Captain Wentworth thus seems to become Louisa's companion.

Just before Anne is due to leave Uppercross in November an excursion to Lyme Regis is arranged, where Captain Harville, an old friend of Captain Wentworth's, lives. Anne, Henrietta and Louisa, Mary, Charles and Captain Wentworth go to Lyme to spend a night in an inn there and to meet Captain Harville, his wife, and his friend Captain Benwick. Captain Benwick was engaged to be married to Captain Harville's sister, Fanny, who had died suddenly the previous summer. He and Anne discuss poetry and she tries to console him. Anne's looks improve with being out in the sea air, and she twice meets a handsome gentleman in Lyme who obviously admires her; Captain Wentworth notices his admiration. He proves to be Mr William Walter Elliot, Sir Walter's heir, whom Elizabeth had hoped to marry. He had, however, married a rich woman for whom he is now in mourning. He leaves Lyme. Anne's party goes for a walk on the harbour wall where Louisa jumps too soon as she is being lifted down steep steps by Captain Wentworth and falls unconscious. Anne remains calm, sending Captain Benwick for a doctor and arranging for Louisa to be carried back to their inn. Louisa is left at the Harvilles' house with Mary and Charles while Anne, Henrietta and Captain Wentworth return to Uppercross to tell Louisa's parents what has happened.

Louisa begins to recover and Anne leaves Uppercross to stay with Lady Russell; she is embarrassed by having to speak of Captain Wentworth to Lady Russell. They move to Bath, though Anne is reluctant to return to her father and sister. She is surprised by the warmth with which they welcome her and she finds that Mr Elliot has re-established his relationship with them. Anne cannot understand why, as he has nothing to gain by it. He calls late in the evening and is amazed that the woman he had admired in Lyme proves to be his cousin. Mrs Clay is still with Elizabeth and has ingratiated herself still further with Sir Walter; Mr Elliot disapproves of this intimacy. Anne thinks he values rank too highly, as her father does; Sir Walter and Elizabeth are full of delight and conceit because they are seen publicly with dull but noble cousins, Viscountess Dalrymple and her daughter, the Honourable Miss Carteret.

Anne re-establishes her friendship with a former school-friend in Bath, Mrs Smith, who is now widowed, poor and crippled. Sir Walter's snobbery is offended by this friendship but Anne perseveres in it. Lady

Russell hopes and expects that Mr Elliot will propose marriage to Anne when he is out of mourning for his first wife, but Anne decides that she could not accept him as she mistrusts his ability to please everyone, and the way in which he conceals his true opinions. She receives a letter from Mary telling her that Louisa is engaged to Captain Benwick. Captain Wentworth arrives in Bath; Anne meets him a shop and he offers to escort her home, but Mr Elliot has already arranged to do so. They meet again at a concert, but again Captain Wentworth is driven away by Mr Elliot's presence; Anne guesses that Captain Wentworth loves her but is jealous of Mr Elliot. She cannot think how to convey her feelings to him.

When Anne next visits Mrs Smith it becomes clear that Mrs Smith expects Anne to marry Mr Elliot. Anne explains that she has no intention of doing so and Mrs Smith then feels free to tell Anne that she knows him to be cold and cruel. He was formerly a friend of her dead husband, and led him into debt; he also confided to them that he thought Sir Walter and Elizabeth ridiculous, and that he married his wife for her money. Mrs Smith has heard indirectly that he now loves Anne, though he renewed his acquaintance with Sir Walter because he wants to prevent him from marrying Mrs Clay and producing a male heir to come between Mr Elliot and the baronetcy. Mr Elliot was executor of Mr Smith's will but refused to act, leaving Mrs Smith almost destitute.

The Musgroves arrive in Bath while Mr Elliot is supposed to be away from Bath on a visit, though Anne sees him with Mrs Clay. Charles Hayter and Henrietta are to marry soon and Henrietta has come to buy clothes for her wedding. Anne visits the Musgroves and meets Captain Wentworth there; Elizabeth calls and invites them all to a party the next evening. The next morning when Anne calls at the Musgroves' hotel again she takes the opportunity to claim that women love as deeply and constantly as men, knowing that she is overheard by Captain Wentworth. He slips a letter to her as he is leaving which says he has never stopped loving her and begs for a reply. They meet outside in the street and tell each other their true feelings, explaining misunderstandings. They meet again, both radiantly happy, at Elizabeth's party; Anne thinks she was right to accept Lady Russell's advice to break off their engagement when she was younger. Captain Wentworth asks whether she would have married him six years earlier when he was promoted. When she says she would, he blames his own pride for not having asked her again as he wanted to.

Anne's relations and friends agree to her marriage with Captain Wentworth but are mortified by the withdrawal of Mr Elliot. He goes to London and establishes Mrs Clay as his mistress there. Anne is humiliated by the inferiority of her own family to that of Captain Wentworth but he soon appreciates the worth of Lady Russell and of Mrs Smith.

He is able to recover some of Mrs Smith's property which gives her more money to live on, and her health improves. Anne has a happy and fulfilled married life.

Detailed summaries

Chapter 1

Sir Walter Elliot is introduced as a handsome, conceited baronet of fifty-four who confirms his sense of his own importance by reading about himself in the Baronetage. His wife, who was a good sensible woman, has died, leaving three daughters, the youngest of whom, Mary, is married to a gentleman, Charles Musgrove. Lady Elliot's friend, Lady Russell, has helped to guide her three daughters since their mother's death; her favourite is Anne, whose looks have faded early. Her father finds her unattractive and prefers his eldest daughter, Elizabeth, who is still a beauty at twenty-nine but is anxious to marry before she begins to age. She had intended to marry her father's heir, Mr William Walter Elliot, but he had married someone else, and although his wife has just died Elizabeth feels humiliated by the fact that she has heard that Mr Elliot mocks her family and she cannot forgive this. A new anxiety is that her father is getting into serious debt and cannot economise. He calls Lady Russell and Mr Shepherd, his agent, to advise him and his daughters on how they can save money without embarrassment.

NOTES AND GLOSSARY:

Somersetshire: a county in the south-west of England
Baronetage: J. Debrett's *Baronetage of England* in two volumes, first published in 1808
earliest patents ... creations of the last century: Sir Walter admires the few surviving baronetcies from the distant past more than those where the first holder of the title was ennobled in the eighteenth century
High Sheriff: high office within a county to which the holder is appointed by royal patent
representing a borough: serving as Member of Parliament
duodecimo: indicates the size of the pages; it means a sheet of paper has been folded four times to make twelve pages; it is therefore a small book
arms and motto: Sir Walter's title also brings with it a coat of arms and a family motto
seat: the family house
valet: personal man servant
crow's foot: ageing lines round the eyes

chaise and four:	a travelling carriage pulled by four horses
leading the way:	Sir Walter and his family are shown to be formal about matters of etiquette; as eldest daughter and mistress of the house Elizabeth takes precedence over most other women
book of books:	the Baronetage
Tattersall's:	a renowned auction-house for horses
black ribbons:	Mr Elliot's wife is dead and he is in mourning
alienable:	able to be sold, separating it from the estate

Chapter 2

Mr Shepherd begs Sir Walter to accept Lady Russell's advice. She, though sensible and honest, is prejudiced in favour of the aristocracy, and is anxious to prevent Sir Walter's economies from being humiliating to him. She consults Anne and they draw up plans for Sir Walter to save money, feeling that his standing in society can only be enhanced by his making savings to pay his debts. He refuses all their suggestions, but agrees to Mr Shepherd's idea that he should leave Kellynch Hall for Bath, though Anne dislikes the thought of leaving home. Lady Russell is keen for Anne to mix in society more and so encourages the move. Sir Walter will not agree to advertising his house for rent and will only let it to an applicant who approaches him directly. Lady Russell is particularly anxious for the family to leave Kellynch, as Elizabeth has formed what she considers to be an unsuitable friendship with Mrs Clay, the daughter of Mr Shepherd, who has returned with her two children to live with her father after an unhappy marriage. Elizabeth, disregarding Lady Russell's advice, makes Mrs Clay her confidante rather than Anne.

NOTES AND GLOSSARY:

zealous:	actively enthusiastic
decorum:	that which is proper
rank and consequence:	Lady Russell admires titles, such as Sir Walter's, which are hereditary. He is a baronet; a knighthood is not hereditary
expedition:	speed
prescribed:	laid down as a rule to be followed
requisitions:	demands
groves:	small woods
Bath:	a fashionable spa in the west of England
engrafted:	incorporated
solicited:	entreated
complaisance:	politeness

Chapter 3

Mr Shepherd suggests to Sir Walter that a naval man may wish to rent Kellynch now that the Napoleonic Wars are over, and he and his daughter recommend sailors as tenants. Sir Walter is reluctant to let his house, or to allow a tenant much freedom in his use of it. He dislikes sailors because many rise in rank quickly, though they are of inferior birth, and take precedence over aristocrats; he also mocks their weather-beaten appearance. Mrs Clay flatters him by saying that few men retain their good looks as well as country gentlemen like him. A naval officer, Admiral Croft, presents himself soon afterwards as a possible tenant of Kellynch Hall, and, as he is married but childless, Mr Shepherd recommends him to Sir Walter, who agrees to meet the Admiral. Mr Shepherd points out that Mrs Croft's brother, a clergyman, once lived near Kellynch. Only Anne can remember that his name was Wentworth. Sir Walter's vanity is sufficiently flattered by the idea of having an admiral as a tenant and he accepts the proposal. This leads Anne to speculate about an unexplained 'he' who will soon be walking in the gardens at Kellynch.

NOTES AND GLOSSARY:

peace:	at the end of the Napoleonic Wars
prize:	Sir Walter is punning here as 'prize' means both reward and anything seized as booty in war
tax:	obligation
utility:	usefulness
personableness:	good looks
rear-admiral of the white:	the lowest of three ranks of admiral in the White Squadron, between the Red and the Blue in seniority. There were 76 rear-admirals in the British Navy at the end of the Napoleonic Wars
Trafalgar:	the British naval victory in 1805, in which Lord Nelson was killed
livery:	uniform worn by servants
the deputation:	the right to shoot game in the manor
trespass:	an encroachment on someone else's property
in the fact:	in the act of trespassing
curacy:	office of assistant clergyman; curates could however sometimes have charge of a parish

Chapter 4

The 'he' was in fact the clergyman's brother, Captain Frederick Wentworth. Anne met him and fell in love with him when he was visiting his brother seven years previously. They had become engaged, but Sir Walter disapproved of the engagement, as did Lady Russell, who wanted Anne to marry a man with more property and social standing. Captain Wentworth seemed headstrong and over-confident to Lady Russell, and she persuaded Anne that it would be in Captain Wentworth's interests as well as hers if she ended the engagement. When Anne did so Captain Wentworth left, feeling that Lady Russell was wrong and that Anne had treated him badly. Anne pined and lost her youthful good looks, and met no one who could have taken Wentworth's place in her affections. Lady Russell was disappointed that she did not accept the proposal of Charles Musgrove, a young man of good family and property, but Anne's sister Mary married him a little later. In fact Captain Wentworth made the progress in his profession that he expected to; he became a captain young, and Anne deduced from reading about him in newspapers that he must have made a lot of money but that he did not seem to have married. She now believes that Lady Russell's advice, though well-meant, was misguided, and that she should have married Captain Wentworth for she has suffered bitter misery at having to renounce him. As she will probably have to meet Captain Wentworth before long she is consoled by the fact that only her own immediate family and Wentworth's brother know of their former relationship, and that the brother no longer lives in the area.

NOTES AND GLOSSARY:

commander:	naval rank above first lieutenant
action:	sea battle, here a battle in the Napoleonic Wars on 6 February 1806
realized:	converted into property
sanguine:	hopeful
deprecated:	expressed disapproval of
rupture:	parting
nice:	discriminating
partialities:	unfairnesses
futurity:	future time
Providence:	God
by successive captures:	officers could make fortunes in wartime from prize money

Chapter 5

Sir Walter and the Admiral like each other well enough to agree about the Admiral's tenancy of Kellynch, and Sir Walter intends to move to Bath early in the autumn. Anne's married sister, Mary, who lives three miles away at Uppercross, writes demanding that Anne should visit her as she is unwell. Lady Russell is perturbed that Mrs Clay is travelling to Bath as a companion for Elizabeth; Anne attempts to make Elizabeth understand that by her flattering manner Mrs Clay may succeed in trapping Sir Walter into marriage. Elizabeth rejects the warning as absurd and leaves for Bath with her father and Mrs Clay. Lady Russell leaves Anne with her sister Mary at Uppercross Cottage immediately afterwards. Mary's is a modern house close to her father-in-law's mansion; the families in the two houses visit each other frequently. Mary claims to Anne that her health is poor; Anne tries to comfort her, as she realises that Mary is not ill but is bored and feels neglected. Mary complains of her two children, her husband and her husband's family, and then begins to feel better. The two sisters go to call on the Musgroves in the Great House. Mr and Mrs Musgrove are kind old-fashioned people; of their large family only Mary's husband, Charles, and two daughters, Henrietta and Louisa, are grown up. The two girls are pretty and lively, but Anne does not envy their high spirits as she values her own quieter but more intelligent and cultivated pleasures.

NOTES AND GLOSSARY:

'This indenture showeth': the beginning of the tenancy agreement drawn up between Sir Walter and the Admiral

his own man: his valet

never set the Thames on fire: a common saying, meaning that he will never do anything extraordinary

Michaelmas: 29 September, an English quarter-day

as a good: as property

yeoman: respectable countryman under the rank of gentleman

'squire: esquire, the principal landowner in a district

casements: windows

indisposition: minor illness

take-leave: Anne has done what her father should have done as the local lord of the manor, and has said goodbye to their tenants and to the people who depend on them for charity

Chapter 6

Anne finds no one at Uppercross much interested in what has been happening at Kellynch and tries to concern herself with their interests instead. Mary complains that she is not treated as she should be, as the daughter of a baronet, by the family in the Great House, while the Musgrove girls grumble to Anne that Mary is too insistent about her rank. The two families spend most mornings and evenings together, when Anne often plays country dances for the younger people and visitors to dance. No one notices her musical ability, but as this has only been appreciated by her mother and Captain Wentworth she is used to the situation and does not mind it. The Crofts move into Kellynch Hall and Mary and Anne call on them. Anne likes Mrs Croft but is disconcerted to hear that Captain Wentworth is to visit her soon. When Mrs Musgrove receives this news she is reminded that her son Dick, who had died two years previously, was once on a ship commanded by a Captain Wentworth. She rereads her son's few letters and confirms this; as she and her husband are depressed by the memories of their son that his letters revive, the family from the Great House comes to be cheered by the family at the Cottage for the evening.

NOTES AND GLOSSARY:
game to guard, and to destroy: this indicates that Mr Musgrove is a gentleman with an estate on which game, such as pheasant, is reared and protected in order to provide good sport during the shooting season
upon the gad: out enjoying herself
precedence of mamma: as a baronet's daughter Mary is entitled to take precedence over her mother-in-law in society, for example, in leading the way out of the dining-room
no voice: she could not sing
likeness: physical resemblance
paid off: when naval officers were not required for action they were kept on half-pay until they were summoned for action again
intelligence: news
Dick: a common abbreviation of Richard
midshipman: rank between naval cadet and sub-lieutenant
frigate: warship carrying between 28 and 60 guns
the school-master: Dick Musgrove was obviously poor at spelling; every ship was officially required to carry a school-master to teach writing, arithmetic and navigation and Captain Wentworth seems to have been concerned that he carried out his task properly

Chapter 7

Captain Wentworth arrives at Kellynch, Mr Musgrove calls on him, and Captain Wentworth returns the call. Anne would have met him at the Great House had not her nephew Charles fallen and dislocated his collar-bone. Captain Wentworth is to dine at the Great House the following day, and, since his son is beginning to recover from his fall,

Charles Musgrove decides to go too. Mary is indignant at the general assumption that she, as his mother, should stay with the sick child, and eventually Anne offers to let her go and stay at home herself. At the dinner Charles invites Captain Wentworth to come shooting with him the next day and he does so; he and Anne meet briefly and she feels relief when the meeting is over, but is disturbed by the strength of her feeling for him. Mary reports that Captain Wentworth has said he finds Anne so altered that he would not have recognised her. Anne is deeply hurt, but admits to herself that the eight years that have destroyed her youthful prettiness have made Captain Wentworth even more glowing and manly. Captain Wentworth had no idea that his comment would be repeated to Anne, but had thought her changed and had not forgiven her for her weakness of character in giving him up. He has not met anyone like her since their engagement but now intends to marry, and is looking for a strong-minded woman with a pleasant manner.

NOTES AND GLOSSARY:

in his cellars:	where he kept his wine
apothecary:	a dispenser of drugs who was used as a doctor
joy of the escape:	from meeting Captain Wentworth
to teaze him:	worry or irritate him
shift:	to manage
nice:	discriminating

Chapter 8

Anne and Captain Wentworth meet frequently now in company; Anne feels that he must remember the past as she does, and regrets their lack of intimacy when they were once so much in sympathy with each other. Now he converses with the Musgrove sisters about life in the Navy, which prompts Mrs Musgrove to reminisce about her dead son. Wentworth describes the success of his first command, the *Asp*, and they go on to talk of his command of the *Laconia* where Richard Musgrove was one of his men. Anne thinks she detects amusement in Captain Wentworth's response to Mrs Musgrove's regrets about her son having left Wentworth's ship, but then he sits beside her and listens sympathetically. Admiral Croft and his brother-in-law disagree about the desirability of having women on board their ships; Mrs Croft travels whenever she can with the Admiral, but Captain Wentworth feels that ships cannot accommodate women comfortably. Mrs Croft tells Mrs Musgrove of the countries she has visited with her husband, and the evening ends with dancing. It seems to Anne that both the Musgrove girls and their cousins, the Hayters, are in love with Captain Wentworth; she overhears one of his partners telling him that Anne never dances. In an awkward encounter between her and Captain Wentworth his cold politeness makes Anne suffer.

NOTES AND GLOSSARY:

the year six:	1806
Navy List:	a gazette listing officers, their ships, promotions etc.
The Admiralty:	the headquarters of naval administration in Britain
sloop:	a small ship of war
pelisse:	a long cloak reaching to the ankles and having arm-holes or sleeves
privateers:	private armed vessels commissioned to seize and plunder enemy shipping
the Great Nation:	France
lost in only a sloop:	as a sloop was a small insignificant ship there would not have been much attention given to its loss or the death of its captain
rate:	class of vessel
non-commissioned class:	not put in commission
sentiment:	tender emotion
man-of-war:	an armed ship
Streights:	the Straits of Gibraltar
Deal:	a harbour town in Kent, in the south-east of England
assizes:	sessions held periodically in each county in England for the administration of justice by judges

Chapter 9

Captain Wentworth stays on with his sister at Kellynch, visiting Uppercross frequently, to the displeasure of Charles Hayter, eldest cousin to the young Musgroves. Their mothers, who are sisters, married men of widely differing social status; Mrs Musgrove now belongs to the highest society in the county but Mrs Hayter's husband has little wealth or social standing. However Charles, her eldest son, has education and refinement. He is a curate, and it is generally expected that he will marry Henrietta Musgrove, but he finds everyone, including Henrietta, obsessed with Captain Wentworth when he returns from a brief absence from home. Mary hopes that Captain Wentworth prefers Henrietta to Louisa as she considers it would demean her to be related to Charles Hayter; Charles Musgrove hopes that Henrietta will marry her cousin, and Louisa marry Captain Wentworth. Charles Hayter is anxious about Henrietta's attitude to him. One morning Captain Wentworth calls at the Cottage to find Anne alone with her sick nephew; their embarrassment is not much relieved by the arrival of Charles Hayter, who will not converse with Captain Wentworth. Anne's little nephew,

Walter, aged two, comes in, climbs on her back as she kneels beside his brother, and refuses to get off. Charles Hayter grumbles at him, but Captain Wentworth releases her gently and carries the little boy away; she is overcome by emotion and hurries off to hide her feelings.

NOTES AND GLOSSARY:

Shropshire: a county in the south-west of England

gig: a light, two-wheeled, one-horse, carriage

in orders: a clergyman

consequence: social importance

hardly in any class: below classification even as yeomen

twenty thousand pounds by the war: in prize money during the Napoleonic Wars

Baronet: like Sir Walter

new creation: see the opening pages of the novel; new baronetcies had not the same impressiveness as ancient ones

take place of me: take precedence in society over Mary who is only the daughter, not the wife, of a baronet

bad connections: relationships which Mary considers socially degrading to her

getting something from the Bishop: being appointed to a parish as its vicar, not just as a curate

freehold: an estate fully owned by the possessor, with no rents or duties to be paid on it

vestibule: entrance-hall

particulars: details

Chapter 10

Anne decides, by observing the young people, that Louisa and Henrietta are infatuated with Captain Wentworth but not yet in love with him, nor he with either of them. Charles Hayter seems to withdraw from competing with Wentworth for Henrietta and does not call at Uppercross for three days. On a fine November day Louisa and Henrietta call for Mary and Anne; as they are setting off for a walk they are joined by Charles Musgrove and Captain Wentworth. They reach Winthrop, Charles Hayter's house, and Charles and Henrietta call on the family while the others rest at the top of the hill above the house. Mary expresses her contempt for the Hayters' social position to Captain Wentworth, who despises her for it. Anne recognises his feeling, though he says nothing. As she sits resting she overhears a conversation between Captain Wentworth and Louisa, who pass in the hedgerow behind her. Captain Wentworth says how much he admires Louisa's firmness of purpose. Louisa tells him how much her family wish Charles

Musgrove had married Anne, not Mary, and goes on to explain that they feel Anne refused Charles because she was persuaded to do so by Lady Russell. Anne is disturbed by Captain Wentworth's interest in her story and soon returns to Mary. Charles and Henrietta return with Charles Hayter, who has evidently been reconciled with Henrietta. This leaves Louisa as clearly the companion for Captain Wentworth, and they walk home. On the way they meet Admiral and Mrs Croft in their gig; Captain Wentworth has noticed that Anne is tired, sees to it that they give her a seat in the gig and helps her in. Anne is touched by his thoughtfulness and listens while the Admiral speculates about when Frederick will marry one of the Musgrove girls.

NOTES AND GLOSSARY:

junction: coincidence

counteracting the sweets of poetical despondence: poets sometimes see autumn as a melancholy time of decay whereas farmers plough ready for next year's spring

conscious: self-conscious

hedge-row: this is described in Austen-Leigh's *Memoir*: it 'does not mean a thin formal line of quickset, but an irregular border of copse-wood and timber, often wide enough to contain within it a winding footpath, or a rough cart track' (Chapter 2)

holly: a prickly evergreen

the listener's proverbial fate: the proverb is that the eavesdropper never hears good of himself

incommoded: made uncomfortable

weasel: a small carnivorous animal sometimes kept for hunting rabbits

sitting down together: as man and wife

spread a little more canvas: a nautical term meaning move more quickly

---

Chapter 11

Just before Anne is due to move back to Kellynch to stay with Lady Russell, Captain Wentworth hears that his old friend Captain Harville has settled at Lyme Regis for the winter. Captain Wentworth is anxious to see him, because his health is poor as a result of being wounded two years earlier. When Captain Wentworth returns from Lyme after a brief visit he persuades all the young people to accompany him on his next visit there. In the middle of November Charles, Mary, Anne, Henrietta and Louisa set off with him and arrange to stay in an inn at Lyme. Captain Wentworth calls on his friend while the others stroll round Lyme; they are soon joined by Captain and Mrs Harville and their friend Captain Benwick who was to have married Captain Harville's sister, had she not died the previous summer. His grief endeared him to the Harvilles and he came to live with them at Lyme for the winter. Anne finds the Harvilles kind and hospitable. Captains Benwick and Harville call on the others at their inn later in the evening and Anne discusses poetry with Captain Benwick, who is still grieving over the death of his fiancée. Anne tries to cheer and console him.

NOTES AND GLOSSARY:

Lyme:	Lyme Regis, a coastal town in Dorset. It was called Lyme until 1774 when it became a Royal borough. The evidence of the text suggests that it was still known as Lyme in 1817
curricle:	a light, two-wheeled carriage
November:	often a cold, wet and foggy month with short days and long nights
Cobb:	the word used to mean pier. At Lyme the Cobb is a long harbour wall that sticks out into the sea; it is wide enough to be walked along and has an upper and a lower level
bathing machines:	people used to bathe from small mobile huts which were moved into the water and in which they changed their clothes
Isle of Wight:	a fairly large island off the south coast of England, famous for its beauty spots
pier:	landing-stage
rooms:	assembly rooms which would be open and full of people during the summer
retirement:	seclusion
give-and-take invitations:	the kind of invitations Sir Walter and Elizabeth give, only to people who entertain them or to people whom they wish to patronise
more, or less:	Anne both admires the Harvilles and is sorry that she has missed the opportunity of being their friend, which she would have been had she married Captain Wentworth
no thoroughfare:	the hotel does not expect visitors in the winter as Lyme is not on a road leading somewhere else and so bringing a passing trade to the town
Marmion, The Lady of the Lake:	poems by Sir Walter Scott (1771–1832)
Giaour, The Bride of Abydos:	poems by Lord Byron (1788–1824)
our best moralists:	probably such eighteenth-century writers as Dr Johnson (1709–84)
seniority of mind:	she has suffered longer than he has

Chapter 12

Anne and Henrietta go for a walk on the sands before breakfast; Anne listens sympathetically as Henrietta expresses her wish that Dr Shirley would retire to Lyme, implying that this would provide an opportunity for Charles Hayter to take his place as a curate. Louisa and Captain Wentworth meet them; as they stroll they pass a handsome gentleman who seems to admire Anne. Captain Wentworth notices this admiration. Anne meets the same man in the inn when they return for breakfast, and is impressed both by his admiration of her appearance and by his good manners. He drives off and a waiter informs them that he is Mr Elliot, and so cousin to Anne and Mary. Mary wants Anne to write to Sir Walter and Elizabeth about the meeting, but Anne is aware of the offence Mr Elliot gave them some years before. The whole party, accompanied by the Harvilles and Captain Benwick, go for a walk round Lyme; Captain Harville walks with Anne and tells her of Benwick's devotion to the dead Fanny Harville and of Captain Wentworth's kindness to them all. They leave the Harvilles and go for a last walk along the Cobb; Louisa jumps too soon in being lifted down the steep steps by Captain Wentworth and falls unconscious. She seems to be dead, and only Anne remains calm in the crisis; she sends Captain Benwick for a doctor and has Louisa carried towards the inn. The Harvilles come out of their house to meet them, insisting that Louisa should be taken there. She is put in the Harvilles' bed and the doctor arrives. He thinks she may recover, as the bruise on her head is her only injury. They decide that Anne should stay, upon Captain Wentworth's particular request, to nurse Louisa with Mrs Harville; Charles also wishes to stay while Captain Wentworth takes Henrietta and Mary back to Mr and Mrs Musgrove. Mary, jealous and selfish, refuses to leave, so she remains with Louisa and Anne reluctantly accompanies Henrietta and Captain Wentworth back to Uppercross. Captain Wentworth consults Anne about what to do next, which gives her pleasure; he returns to Lyme while she remains at Uppercross with the Musgroves.

NOTES AND GLOSSARY:
seizure: sudden attack of illness
a dispensation: become an absentee clergyman
They were all at her disposal: they all (politely) agreed to her suggestion
arms and livery: both would indicate Mr Elliot's ancestry
made into the Grappler: given orders to join the *Grappler*
run up to the yard-arm: hanged
leave of absence: permission to be absent
per force: of necessity
jar: jolt

lifeless:	unconscious
temples:	forehead
salts:	smelling salts
surgeon:	doctor
insensible:	unconscious
animate:	enliven
cordials:	medicines
restoratives:	medicines
contusion:	bruise

the time required by the Uppercross horses: a coach would not travel as fast as a chaise

Emma towards her Henry: this refers to a poem *Henry and Emma* by Matthew Prior (1664–1721). In it Emma says she is willing to serve a woman with whom Henry pretends he is in love

baited: given food and drink

Chapter 13

The family at Uppercross receives news that Louisa is improving slowly; they send their old nursemaid to look after her. They are distressed that Anne is about to leave to stay with Lady Russell, and all decide to move to Lyme to stay near Louisa until she can return home. Anne is left alone for an hour, feeling lonely, until Lady Russell's carriage arrives to take her to Kellynch. She is embarrassed at having to speak of Captain Wentworth with Lady Russell, as she describes what has happened to Louisa, but finds it easier when she has explained the love she assumes exists between Louisa and Captain Wentworth. Lady Russell is pleased to think that she was right about Captain Wentworth's character. She takes Anne on a courtesy visit to the Crofts at Kellynch; Anne feels that the Crofts deserve to live at Kellynch more than her family do. Captain Wentworth has called there and enquired particularly about her, and then returned to Lyme. The Crofts are warm and kind to Anne and she is amused when the Admiral expresses his horror at the number of mirrors in his dressing-room, which was Sir Walter's. He has had them all removed. As the Crofts are about to visit relations in the north, the danger that Anne may meet Captain Wentworth, or that Lady Russell and Captain Wentworth may meet, is removed.

NOTES AND GLOSSARY:

blains:	blisters
tenements:	houses
plaister:	plaster

Chapter 14

Mary and Charles visit Anne as soon as they return to Uppercross, reporting that Louisa is better but still too weak to be moved. Mary has enjoyed herself in Lyme, but is jealous when Charles says that Captain Benwick would have visited them at the Cottage had Anne still been living at Uppercross. Mary abuses Captain Benwick for his dullness and bookishness, while Anne and Charles defend him to Lady Russell, who makes clear her disapproval of Mr Elliot. Charles expects Captain Benwick to visit Anne, as he refused to go to Plymouth with Captain Wentworth, but he does not come. The Musgroves return without Louisa to Uppercross but with the Harvilles' children, to welcome their younger children home from school for Christmas. Their house is lively and noisy and they are looking forward to Louisa's return with the Harvilles soon after Christmas. Lady Russell disapproves of the noise at Uppercross, though she enjoys an equal degree of noise when she arrives in Bath a few days later with Anne. Anne dislikes being in Bath though she knows Mr Elliot has reconciled himself with Elizabeth and Sir Walter. Lady Russell leaves Anne to stay at her father's house in Camden Place and goes on to her own lodgings.

NOTES AND GLOSSARY:
paid their compliments: made a courtesy call
tressels: tables
brawn: potted meat
drays: low carts
pattens: wooden over-shoes
muffin-men: sellers of muffins, light spongy cakes
branch . . . tree: the metaphor is the family tree, of which Mr Elliot is a branch

Chapter 15

Anne enters her father's elegant house reluctantly, but is surprised by the warmth of the welcome her father and sisters give her, though this is caused mainly by their pleasure in finding someone new to whom to show off their house and furniture. They are happy about the social esteem in which they are held, and that Mr Elliot has re-established his relationship with them. He has assured them of his respect for them and his friend Colonel Wallis has explained to them that Mr Elliot married because his wife had been beautiful, and rich, and had pursued Mr Elliot, being deeply in love with him. Anne cannot understand why Mr Elliot has become reconciled with them after so many years of ignoring them, as he has nothing to gain by it; he is rich and the baronetcy and estate will be his when Sir Walter dies. She thinks he must be attracted by Elizabeth. They spend the evening talking of Mr Elliot, and of the appearance of Sir Walter's acquaintances. At ten o'clock Mr Elliot calls, and is astonished that the woman he admired at Lyme proves to be his cousin. Anne finds his manners comparable only with Captain Wentworth's. They talk of Lyme, and when he leaves at eleven Anne is amazed that her first evening with her family has passed so pleasantly.

NOTES AND GLOSSARY:

complaisance: desire to please

having cards left: when people made formal calls and the host was out they left visiting cards to show that they had called; this could be used as a way of initiating a social relationship

unfeudal: not supporting the old values of hereditary rights and privileges for the aristocracy and gentry

under-hung: having the lower jaw projecting beyond the upper

foot-boy: servant

'eleven with its silver sounds': an untraced quotation

watchman: the man who walked the streets of the town all night calling out the time on the hour and acting as a kind of policeman; the police force was formed in 1839

Chapter 16

Anne is anxious that her father may be in love with Mrs Clay, whom he has urged to stay on with them. Elizabeth seems not to notice his admiration of her. He compliments Anne on her improved appearance and compares it to the (imagined) improvement in Mrs Clay's complexion. Lady Russell is also vexed by this kind of praise; she admires Mr Elliot more than Anne does but Anne recognises that they differ. Anne thinks that he values rank too highly, as her own family does. This is made evident when the Dowager Viscountess Dalrymple and her daughter, the Hon. Miss Carteret, arrive in Bath. They are noble cousins of the Elliots, but were estranged some years before. Sir Walter writes an extravagant letter to the Viscountess and she replies that she will be happy to meet the Elliots. Anne is ashamed by the ostentation of the relationship; she finds the Viscountess and her daughter superior in nothing but birth, and argues with Mr Elliot that the relationship with them is meaningless, though he values it because of their rank. He, however, agrees with Anne that Mrs Clay's influence on Sir Walter should be curbed.

Gowland: R.W. Chapman in his notes quotes an advertisement that appeared in *The Bath Chronicle* on 6 January 1814 for Mrs Vincent's Gowland's Lotion to remedy any skin condition

drinks the water: the water in Bath is reputed to have medicinal qualities

crape round his hat: a sign that he is in mourning for his wife

Dowager Viscountess: the widow of a Viscount

Honourable: a prefix given to the sons and daughters of peers below the rank of Marquess

letter of condolence: a formal letter commiserating with the Viscountess which should have been sent on the death of the Viscount

Laura-place: a fashionable address

first set in Bath: the social élite

a little learning: a quotation from the *Essay on Criticism* by Alexander Pope (1688–1744)

Chapter 17

Anne hears that a woman named Mrs Smith, who was kind to her when they were both school-girls, is in Bath; she is widowed, poor and crippled. She has come to Bath to take the medicinal waters, and Anne visits her in her humble lodgings. They quickly re-establish their former friendly relationship; Anne admires her cheerfulness in the face of loneliness, suffering and hardship. Mrs Smith's husband had been wealthy but extravagant, and left his financial affairs so confused that his widow had little money to live on. Mrs Smith tells Anne how much she values the kindness of her nurse, Nurse Rooke, who cares for her and teaches her how to knit and to make small objects which the nurse then sells to her wealthy clients, enabling Mrs Smith to give a little money to very poor families living nearby. Anne assumes that Nurse Rooke sees the heroic side of human nature in visiting the sick; Mrs Smith thinks she may see the weak and selfish side. She tells Anne that Nurse Rooke is currently attending Mrs Wallis, whom Anne knows to be the wife of Colonel Wallis, a friend of Mr Elliot's. Sir Walter is disgusted when he discovers that Anne is visiting a woman with a common name and a humble address, though Anne privately considers that there is little social distinction to be made between Mrs Smith and Mrs Clay. Lady Russell approves of Anne's visits to Mrs Smith and tells her how much Mr Elliot admires her compassion. Lady Russell thinks that Mr Elliot may propose marriage to Anne when he is out of mourning for his first wife, and tells Anne what pleasure it would give her to see Anne as

Lady Elliot, in her mother's former position. Anne is momentarily swayed by this idea but immediately realises that she could never accept Mr Elliot as he is too generally pleasing and does not give away his real opinions and feelings.

NOTES AND GLOSSARY:

rheumatic fever: an acute disease causing fever and pain and swelling in the joints

protegée: someone under the care of another

the warm bath: one of the public baths in Bath, which were originally constructed by the Romans

no honours: an honourable addition could be made to a coat of arms as a reward for a special achievement

Chapter 18

Anne, early in February, receives a letter from Mary brought by Admiral and Mrs Croft, who have just arrived in Bath. The letter is full of contradictory complaints, but also contains the news that the Harvilles and Louisa have just returned to Uppercross and that Louisa is to marry Captain Benwick. Anne is amazed but thinks they will be happy; she rejoices that Captain Wentworth and Louisa can no longer be assumed to be in love. Sir Walter decides that he cannot introduce the Crofts to his noble cousin Lady Dalrymple, but the Crofts are happy and have all the friends they want in Bath. Anne meets the Admiral, who tells her the news of Louisa's engagement; she pretends not to know it and asks whether Captain Wentworth is distressed by the engagement. The Admiral thinks Captain Wentworth should be brought to Bath to find a wife.

NOTES AND GLOSSARY:

with Admiral and Mrs Croft's compliments: this means that the Admiral had conveyed the letter from Uppercross to Bath for Mary

make my letter as long as I like: she will not have to pay for it according to its weight

gout: a form of rheumatism usually associated with old men

cockleshell: small frail boat

three shilling piece: D.W. Harding, in the notes to the Penguin edition of *Persuasion*, explains that the Bank of England issued three shilling token coins between 1811 and 1816 to relieve the shortage of silver caused by the Napoleonic Wars

younker: young man
Peace has come too soon: the Wars ended before the grandson was old enough to go to sea and try for prize money and promotion
piano: quiet

Chapter 19

Captain Wentworth arrives in Bath; Anne first sees him when she, her sister, Mrs Clay and Mr Elliot have been caught in a shower. Elizabeth and Mrs Clay are to be taken home in Lady Dalrymple's barouche while Anne and Mr Elliot are to walk. As the ladies are waiting in a shop for Mr Elliot to return from an errand, Captain Wentworth enters with a group of people, and is obviously embarrassed by meeting Anne. Elizabeth refuses to acknowledge him. He offers to accompany Anne home but at this moment Mr Elliot reappears and leads Anne away. When she has gone, the ladies in Captain Wentworth's party comment favourably on Anne's looks and on the likelihood of an engagement between her and Mr Elliot. Anne waits anxiously for Lady Russell and Captain Wentworth to meet; she and Anne pass him one morning, and Anne thinks Lady Russell is studying him closely, but she is in fact looking out for some particularly fine curtains she has been told about. Anne looks forward to a concert where she expects to meet Captain Wentworth again. She visits Mrs Smith who says she expects that Anne's visits to her will soon stop, implying that Anne will soon marry.

NOTES AND GLOSSARY:
Mollands: Chapman records that the Bath Directory for 1812 has 'Molland Mrs, Cook and confectioner, 2, Milson-street'
barouche: a four-wheeled carriage
arch: pleasantly mischievous
chair: a sedan chair, an enclosed seat for one person carried on poles by two bearers, one in front and one behind

---

Chapter 20

Captain Wentworth arrives early at the concert; this time both Sir Walter and Elizabeth acknowledge him. He talks to Anne with increasing animation, making clear that he thinks Louisa an ordinary though pleasant girl, and feels that Benwick ought not to have recovered from his grief for Fanny Harville and become engaged to Louisa so quickly. Much of what he says reflects on his own former relationship with Anne.

The Dalrymples' party arrives and Anne has to greet them, but she enters the concert room glowing with happiness. She sits next to Mr Elliot who flatters her during the interval and implies that he would like to marry her; he says he knew her by reputation long before he met her but refuses to say how. Anne hears Lady Dalrymple and Sir Walter commenting on Captain Wentworth's good looks and hopes he will come nearer, particularly as she is distressed by Mr Elliot's flattery. During the second interval she manages to move to the end of a bench, and Captain Wentworth does come to speak to her, but he seems constrained, and, when Mr Elliot talks to her, Captain Wentworth says there is nothing worth staying for and leaves. Anne realises that he loves her and is jealous of Mr Elliot, but does not know how to convey her own feelings to him.

NOTES AND GLOSSARY:

the rooms, the octagon room: the assembly rooms where people met in Bath, and where such events as concerts were held

concert bill: a programme

the gapes: yawns

Miss Larolles: Harding quotes a passage from the novel *Cecilia* (1782) by Fanny Burney (1752–1840) spoken by a Miss Larolles, 'It's the shockingest thing you can conceive, to be made to sit in the middle of those forms; one might as well be at home, for nobody can speak to one'

Chapter 21

Anne visits Mrs Smith next morning, partly to avoid meeting Mr Elliot. Anne can tell little about the concert, which leads Mrs Smith to suppose that she was preoccupied by the man she loves. Anne cannot think how she has guessed this, but it becomes clear that Mrs Smith thinks Anne is about to become engaged to Mr Elliot, and wants Anne to intercede with him on her behalf, as she thinks he can help her. When Anne makes it clear that she has no intention of marrying Mr Elliot, Mrs Smith declares that she has decided to tell Anne all she knows about him, saying that he is cold, designing and cruel. When she was first married she and her husband, who was then wealthy, were close friends of Mr Elliot, rather a poor law student. They were generous to him, and he confided to them that he intended to make his fortune by marrying a rich wife; he withdrew at that time from his relationship with Sir Walter's family because Elizabeth was not wealthy enough for him. Mrs Smith spoke with him also of Anne, which explains how Mr Elliot knew her by reputation before he met her. Mr Elliot's wife was his social inferior, and he married her only because she was rich. At that time he was indifferent to his claims to the Kellynch title and estate, as Mrs Smith proves to Anne by showing her a letter he wrote then to her husband. It states his intention of selling Kellynch as soon as he inherits it. Mrs Smith has heard from Mrs Rooke who attends Mrs Wallis, the wife of Mr Elliot's great friend, that Mr Elliot loves Anne and wants to marry her, though he first renewed his acquaintance with Sir Walter's family because he now wants the title of baronet and is afraid Sir Walter may marry Mrs Clay and produce a new heir to the baronetcy. He thinks Mrs Clay is frightened of him and consequently has less influence over Sir Walter. Mrs Smith then tells Anne how Mr Elliot, after he had become rich through his marriage, led her husband into extravagance which he could not afford; he died before he realised that he was financially ruined, and left Mr Elliot as executor of his will. Mr Elliot refused to act, leaving Mrs Smith in financial hardship which might have been alleviated had property of her husband's in the West Indies been recovered. But she is too frail and poor, and Mr Elliot too selfish to do anything about it, and she has no relations to help her. She had hoped that, had Anne married Mr Elliot, he might have been persuaded to help her. Anne shudders to think how much Lady Russell wants her to marry Mr Elliot and leaves, intending to tell Lady Russell what she has discovered.

NOTES AND GLOSSARY:

chambers in the Temple: rooms in one of the two Inns of Court in London, meaning that Mr Elliot was training for the law

farthing: the coin of lowest value then current in England

grazier: one who feeds cattle for market

The stream . . . away: my information is indirect but correct, and soon cleared of inaccuracies

executor of his will: the person who carries out the conditions of the will

sequestration: an order of court which resulted in the seizing of some of Mr Smith's property so that the liabilities incurred by the property could be paid from it

Chapter 22

When Anne arrives home she finds that she has missed Mr Elliot's morning visit; Mrs Clay is busy flattering Elizabeth by saying that Mr Elliot visits them so often for Elizabeth's sake. He returns in the evening and Anne is coolly polite to him. He is to leave Bath on a visit to friends the next morning, and to stay away two days. Anne plans to visit Lady

Russell that morning, but is prevented by the arrival of Charles and Mary, who are in Bath with Mrs Musgrove, Henrietta, and Captain Harville. Charles tells Anne that Charles Hayter has received an appointment in the Church, and so is in a position to marry Henrietta; his parents are pleased though Mary is not. He reports that Louisa is better, but nervous and quiet. Elizabeth invites Mary and Charles to a party the next evening to meet Lady Dalrymple, Miss Carteret and Mr Elliot, and they agree, leaving with Anne to call on Mrs Musgrove and Henrietta.

They greet Anne warmly and welcome a lively succession of callers, including Captain Wentworth. Mary draws Anne's attention to the fact that Mr Elliot and Mrs Clay are talking and shaking hands outside the window, though Mr Elliot is supposed to be off visiting friends at this time. Anne is embarrassed by the smiles exchanged between the ladies present at the mention of Mr Elliot; there is obviously an assumption, which Captain Wentworth may share, that she is about to become engaged to him. Charles informs his mother that he has booked a box for them all at the theatre for the next evening, but Mary is furious, as this is the time of Elizabeth's party. Anne, aware of Captain Wentworth, makes clear that she would rather go to the play with the Musgroves than meet Mr Elliot at the party. Captain Wentworth moves across to speak to Anne, but they are interrupted by the arrival of Sir Walter and Elizabeth who distribute invitations to everyone, including Captain Wentworth, to their party; the date of the visit to the theatre is to be altered. Anne is again embarrassed, this time by Sir Walter's and Elizabeth's cold formality; everyone is relieved when they leave. Anne is exhausted, and returns home wondering whether Captain Wentworth intends to come to the party. She lets Mrs Clay know that she was seen with Mr Elliot and thinks that Mrs Clay looks guilty for a moment.

NOTES AND GLOSSARY:

éclat:	(*French*) ostentation
arrangé:	(*French*) pre-arranged, studied
blinds:	screens over windows
shooting was over:	the shooting season was over
daughters' shares:	dowry
does not above half like:	does not much like
dab chick:	a small water bird that ducks under water for food
colonnade:	a row of columns with a roof over them
box:	a separate compartment in a theatre with seats in it, often close to the sides of the stage
neglect . . . sun:	a metaphor meaning that Charles will not curry favour with the heir to the title while the title is held by Mary's father

Chapter 23

Anne arrives at the Musgroves' lodgings the next morning to find Mrs Croft and both Captain Harville and Captain Wentworth there. Mrs Croft and Mrs Musgrove are agreeing that long or uncertain engagements are a bad thing; Anne looks up and finds Captain Wentworth glancing at her, as this comment applies to their former relationship. Captain Harville engages Anne in conversation about the relative constancy in love of men and women; a miniature of Captain Benwick painted for Captain Harville's sister, Fanny, but now being framed for Louisa, causes him to reflect regretfully on the speed with which Captain Benwick recovered from his grief for Fanny Harville. Anne claims that women love as deeply and constantly as men, knowing that, as she speaks, she is overheard by Captain Wentworth. Soon afterwards he leaves abruptly with Captain Harville, but, returning for his gloves, he places a letter addressed to her in front of her and leaves again. In it she reads that he has never ceased to love her and begs for a response from her. She is so agitated that she looks ill, and everyone in the room wants to help her; eventually Charles offers to accompany her home. They are overtaken by Captain Wentworth whom Charles asks to escort her, as he has an engagement. Anne and Captain Wentworth are delighted and, as soon as they are left alone, speak of their true feelings. Captain Wentworth has indeed been jealous of Mr Elliot and never loved Louisa, though he only realised gradually how much he loved Anne and how superior to Louisa she was. After Louisa's engagement, when he considered himself free of any obligation to her, he went immediately to Bath to see Anne. Anne reaches home almost afraid of her own happiness; at the evening party she is radiantly happy and lovely. In an interval alone with Captain Wentworth she claims that she was right, when they were first engaged, to be guided by Lady Russell's advice; he asks whether she would have accepted him six years before when he had made money and succeeded in his career. When she replies that she would have, he blames his own pride for not asking her then, when he wanted to.

NOTES AND GLOSSARY:

the Sultaness Scheherazade's head: each night, for a thousand and one nights, she told stories, breaking off at the most interesting points, in order to be allowed to live the next day

miniature painting: before the days of photographs it was a common practice for people to carry about miniature portraits of their loved ones

anchorage: a naval joke meaning that he likes his position

hers in honour: since everyone supposed him to be in love with Louisa it would have been dishonourable for him to withdraw from his relationship with her though he himself did not want it

Chapter 24

Anne's relations agree to her marriage with Captain Wentworth; Lady Russell acknowledges that she has mistaken the characters of Captain Wentworth and of Mr Elliot. Elizabeth is mortified by Mr Elliot's withdrawal, particularly as he left Bath and was followed to London by Mrs Clay; she has become his mistress, but may become his wife. Anne is humiliated by the inferiority of her own family to Captain Wentworth's, but he soon becomes attached to her two friends, Lady Russell and Mrs Smith. He writes letters on Mrs Smith's behalf and recovers her husband's property in the West Indies which gives her more money to live on, and at the same time her health improves. Anne is happy and fulfilled in her married life, and loved and respected by her husband; her one fear is that he will be involved in the naval action if there is another war.

NOTES AND GLOSSARY:
his brothers and sisters: he had only one of each but this includes his brother- and sister-in-law

Part 3

Commentary

The nature of the novel

The nature of Jane Austen's novels did, and does, cause controversy; there are distinguished writers who think her themes trivial and her scope limited. An example of the conflicting reponses her novels evoke can be found in the letters of Charlotte Brontë (1816–55) to the distinguished critic G.H. Lewes. In a letter to him on 12 January 1848 she writes:

> What induced you to say that you would have rather written 'Pride and Prejudice' or 'Tom Jones', than any of the Waverley Novels?
> I had not seen 'Pride and Prejudice', till I read that sentence of yours, and then I got the book. And what did I find? An accurate daguerreotyped portrait of a common-place face; a carefully fenced, highly cultivated garden, with neat borders and delicate flowers; but no glance of a bright, vivid physiognomy, no open country, no fresh air, no blue hill, no bonny beck. I should hardly like to live with her ladies and gentlemen, in their elegant but confined houses.*

He obviously replied immediately, for she writes again on 18 January:

> Then you add, I *must* 'learn to acknowledge her as *one of the greatest artists, of the greatest painters of human character* . . . that ever lived.' . . . Can there be a great artist without poetry? . . . Miss Austen being, as you say, without 'sentiment', without *poetry*, maybe *is* sensible, real (more *real* than *true*), but she cannot be great.†

Charlotte Brontë goes to the central critical question about Jane Austen: can a writer who is so restricted in her subject matter be, as Lewes claimed, one of 'the greatest painters of human character'? In one sense Anne Elliot's story is comparable with that of Charlotte Brontë's Jane Eyre; both renounce the men they love because their consciences will not allow them to continue the relationship, and both are rewarded by their authors eventually, by being reunited with the loved ones. Both have offers of marriage after their renunciation which they reject for love of the seemingly unattainable first men. There the

---

*Elizabeth Gaskell: *The Life of Charlotte Brontë*, Smith, Elder and Co., London, 1857, Chapter 16, p.352
†*Life of Charlotte Brontë*, Chapter 16, p.353

resemblance ends and it is almost absurd to make any connection between the two novels, as the world each novelist creates for her heroine to inhabit is so different from the other. Jane Eyre is a witty young woman, but it would be foolish to call the novel *Jane Eyre* primarily a comic novel. What we are made to feel most strongly in it are Jane Eyre's isolation and agony; the physical setting often interacts with the characters, embodying their emotional and spiritual states. Although as readers we do not question the strength of Anne Elliot's feeling for Captain Wentworth, we are not invited to participate in its misery by the author; *Persuasion* is a novel about the way in which human beings behave in society. Is it therefore 'more *real* than *true*' as Charlotte Brontë claims?

She seems to mean by this that the inclusion of the detail of everyday life, the letter-writing, visiting, and piano-playing that are a significant part of our picture of Anne Elliot, obscures what is the emotional truth of the situation, that Anne yearns for Captain Wentworth. A different view from an author whom Charlotte Brontë and Jane Austen admired intensely, Sir Walter Scott, shows that he felt that the commonplace details included in Jane Austen's writing were what made her remarkable as a novelist:

> The Big Bow-wow strain I can do myself like any now going; but the exquisite touch, which renders ordinary commonplace things and characters interesting, from the truth of the description and the sentiment, is denied to me.*

She herself refused to be tempted out of the limits she imposed on herself, as she shows in a letter to the Prince Regent's librarian, James Stanier Clarke:

> I am fully sensible that an historical romance, founded on the House of Saxe Cobourg, might be much more to the purpose of profit or popularity than such pictures of domestic life in country villages as I deal in. But I could no more write a romance than an epic poem. I could not sit seriously down to write a serious romance under any other motive than to save my life; and if it were indispensable for me to keep it up and never relax into laughing at myself or other people, I am sure I should be hung before I had finished the first chapter. No, I must keep to my own style and go on in my own way; and though I may never succeed again in that, I am convinced that I should totally fail in any other.†

Journal, 14 March 1826, quoted (from *The Journal of Sir Walter Scott*, Edinburgh, 1890) in Andrew Wright, *Jane Austen's Novels*, Chatto and Windus, London, 1953
†*Letters*, 1 April 1816, pp.452–3

That she enjoyed the restrictions she imposed on herself is evident from a letter that she wrote to her niece, Anna, about the niece's attempt at novel-writing:

> You are now collecting your People delightfully, getting them exactly into such a spot as is the delight of my life;—3 or 4 Families in a Country Village is the very thing to work on.‡

Her letters to her nephews and nieces show us a good deal about her own methods of working, and are indirectly a response to the kinds of criticisms Charlotte Brontë made of her work. Edward, her nephew, had lost two and a half chapters of his latest novel:

> It is well that *I* have not been at Steventon lately, & therefore cannot be suspected of purloining them;—two strong twigs & a half towards a Nest of my own, would have been something.—I do not think however that any theft of that sort would be really very useful to me. What should I do with your strong, manly, spirited Sketches, full of Variety and Glow?—How could I possibly join them on to the little bit (two Inches wide) of Ivory on which I work with so fine a Brush, as produces little effect after much labour?*

The whole of this letter is, by implication, a defence of her fine brush-work; earlier on she suggests that she and Edward should include some of her brother Henry's 'very superior Sermons' in their novels as 'it would be a fine help to a volume' if they made 'our Heroine read it aloud of a Sunday Evening' as Scott does in *The Antiquary* (1816). She finds such interpolations amusing but sees her own artistry as lying in her fidelity to her fine brushwork, without depending on dramatic incidents and 'spirited sketches'. Both the metaphors she uses, the nest and the little bit of ivory, suggest careful deliberate construction and inter-weaving.

The task she sets herself is to elicit significance from a realistic depiction of a small group of people living ordinary lives like her own. Unlike Scott and many of the great Victorian novelists, she does not set her novel in the past and she does not deal with significant social and political events. She is ironic but not usually satirical; only in *Northanger Abbey* has she one specific target which she intends to ridicule. Her characters' emotions are ordinary, unlike the elemental passion of Heathcliff for Catherine which Emily Brontë (1818–48) creates in *Wuthering Heights* (1847), or the extraordinary fortitude of Jeanie Deans in Scott's *The Heart of Midlothian* (1818). Her characters do live in 'elegant but confined houses' and they are commonplace; what the reader must decide for himself is whether her manipulation of the

‡*Letters*, 9 September 1814, p.401
*Letters, 16 December 1816, pp.468–9

characters gives their behaviour an artistic significance that the comparable real-life situation lacks, whether the author can elicit the 'true' from her presentation of the 'real'.

It is not as easy as it might at first seem to create the 'real'; in *Persuasion* the reader's credulity is stretched by the conclusion. Mrs Smith's role is rather a mechanical one, and the meeting between Mrs Clay and Mr Elliot in Chapter 22 which is made to seem sinister to the reader has no outcome in the following chapters. These are minor flaws however. The 'truth of the description' of 'the involvements, and feelings, and characters of ordinary life', which Scott so much admired and Charlotte Brontë despised, did not come as naturally to Jane Austen as it seems to have done. A chapter of the original draft of *Persuasion* exists and has been republished (for example, in the Penguin edition of the novel); in the finished version Chapters 22 and 23 were substituted for it. A close comparison between the two versions shows how carefully she worked to attain the natural, unforced quality of her plot and characterisation; much of her advice to her nephews and nieces on their attempts at fiction is concerned with the detail of characterisation and whether it is credible:

> Mrs F is not careful enough of Susan's health;—Susan ought not to be walking out so soon after Heavy rains, taking long walks in the dirt. An anxious Mother would not suffer it.*

In the original chapter† Anne meets Admiral Croft in the street, and is invited to call on his wife. Mrs Croft is engaged with her mantua-maker but Captain Wentworth is in the sitting-room; leaving Anne there, the Admiral takes Captain Wentworth outside the door and Anne overhears a lively discussion about which of them is to ask her a question, and eventually Captain Wentworth agrees to do it. He re-enters; he and Anne are intensely embarrassed but he asks whether she is to marry Mr Elliot as rumour suggests and, if so, whether she wishes the Admiral to give up the tenancy of Kellynch Hall. She assures him that she has no intention of marrying Mr Elliot and this leads to their reconciliation, with much of the material that is used in the final version of Chapter 23. It is surprisingly disturbing to a reader who knows *Persuasion* to read this alternative version, because Chapters 22 and 23 are so delicately and convincingly written that the reader feels that was what actually happened. That it only happened that way because Jane Austen thought about, revised and refined the final chapters show the effort and brilliance that lies behind the apparently easy naturalistic detail.

Letters, 9 September 1814, p.401
†There is a detailed comparison between the original chapter of *Persuasion* and those substituted for it in B.C. Southam, *Jane Austen's Literary Manuscripts*, Clarendon Press, Oxford, 1964

There are aspects of character which do not ring true in the cancelled chapter; Mrs Croft is such a sensible, unassuming woman that it is hard to believe that she would spend over half-an-hour with her mantua-maker, and the Admiral's insensitivity in insisting on finding out whether Anne is engaged seems uncharacteristic of him. Anne herself seems more of an adolescent girl and less a mature woman whom the reader would respect; the narrator's tone suggests a complaint more appropriate for Mary than Anne:

> She was almost bewildered—almost too happy in looking back. It was necessary to sit up half the night, and lie awake the remainder, to comprehend with composure her present state, and pay for the overplus of bliss by headache and fatigue.

The tone of this changes radically in the final version, suggesting that Anne can control her happiness as she controlled her grief:

> All the surprise and suspense, and every other painful part of the morning dissipated by this conversation, she re-entered the house so happy as to be obliged to find an alloy in some momentary appre-hensions of its being impossible to last. An interval of meditation, serious and grateful, was the best corrective of every thing dangerous in such high-wrought felicity; and she went to her room, and grew steadfast and fearless in the thankfulness of her enjoyment. (Chapter 23)

The most significant differences between the two versions are that in the first the reconciliation comes about by chance, and without the presence of that group of people which has tested Anne's qualities and brought her to a decision about how to act. In the first version neither hero nor heroine decides to make their feelings known once more:

> To have it burst on her that she was to be the next moment in the same room with him! No time for recollection! for planning behaviour or regulating manners! There was time only to turn pale before she had passed through the door, and met the astonished eyes of Captain Wentworth, who was sitting by the fire, pretending to read, and prepared for no greater surprise than the Admiral's hasty return.

In the final version Anne takes the initiative when she knows that Captain Wentworth is listening to her, and speaks to Captain Harville of women's fidelity in general, referring by implication specifically to her own:

> 'All the privilege I claim for my own sex (it is not a very enviable one, you need not covet it) is that of loving longest, when existence or when hope is gone.' (Chapter 23)

This precipitates the climax; Captain Wentworth responds to it by writing to her:

> 'I can listen no longer in silence. I must speak to you by such means as are within my reach. You pierce my soul . . . I offer myself to you again with a heart even more your own, than when you almost broke it eight years and a half ago. Dare not say that man forgets sooner than woman, that his love has an earlier death. I have loved none but you.' (Chapter 23)

The maturity of this love is communicated to the reader only by the second version; Anne has an adult understanding that trivial mishaps can destroy loving relationships:

> 'Our hearts must understand each other ere long. We are not boy and girl, to be captiously irritable, misled by every moment's inadvertence, and wantonly playing with our own happiness.' And yet, a few minutes afterwards, she felt as if their being in company with each other, under their present circumstances, could only be exposing them to inadvertencies and misconstructions of the most mischievous kind. (Chapter 22)

The inclusion in the scene at the White Hart of so many other characters, and particularly of Captain Harville, heightens the reader's awareness of the seriousness of the novel. Unlike *Pride and Prejudice*, *Persuasion* is not a light-hearted love story; we do not feel that it is inevitable that Anne and Captain Wentworth will marry, and they are seen as exceptional in their fidelity and integrity. They earn their happiness but, because of the redrafted penultimate chapter, we are made aware that happiness in love is a precarious business. Captain Harville has been given a miniature of Captain Benwick which was painted for Captain Benwick's first fiancée, Captain Harville's dead sister Fanny:

> 'I now have the charge of getting it properly set for another! It was a commission to me! But who else was there to employ? I hope I can allow for him . . . Poor Fanny! she would not have forgotten him so soon!' (Chapter 23)

It is appropriate that the reconciliation should be brought about in a crowded room; there is as little privacy in *Persuasion* as Jane Austen herself had for writing her novels. Instead of leaving her lovers alone together in a room, as she did in the first version, Jane Austen even shows their re-engagement as taking place with other people's lives going on around them:

> And there, as they slowly paced the gradual ascent, heedless of every group around them, seeing neither sauntering politicians, bustling

house-keepers, flirting girls, nor nursery-maids and children, they could indulge in those retrospections and acknowledgements, and especially in those explanations of what had directly preceded the present moment, which were so poignant. (Chapter 23)

There is certainly no romantic isolation in this; the momentous events in most readers' own lives take place in ordinary streets or houses and not on moors, lonely crags or in ruined castles. Jane Austen sets herself the deliberate limit of asking the reader to recognise in her fiction places, people and experiences he knows; if she makes a mistake the reader can perceive it through his own experience. A study of the cancelled chapter of *Persuasion* shows that this is not easy. The following sections explore whether Jane Austen in *Persuasion* is able to give the reader more than the pleasure of recognition, which is considerable in itself; whether she provides an insight into the nature of human experience which transcends the particular time and place at which the novel was written and in which it was set.

Structure

Narrative method

As human beings we perceive the world through one pair of eyes only; in *Middlemarch* (1872) George Eliot (1819–80) reminds us of the fact and tells us that she wants us to transcend this limitation and see from Casaubon's point of view as well as from Dorothea's, from Mr Bulstrode's as well as from Lydgate's. In *Persuasion* Jane Austen heightens the realism of the novel by restricting the reader's vision almost entirely to one pair of eyes, and one sensibility. Although she does not use a first person narration Jane Austen rarely tells the reader anything that Anne does not know. There is only one instance where the narrator gives us inside information about what Captain Wentworth is thinking and feeling. At the end of Chapter 7, when Captain Wentworth has just met Anne again after eight years, Jane Austen tells us his response:

He had been most warmly attached to her, and had never seen a woman since whom he thought her equal; but, except from some natural sensation of curiosity, he had no desire of meeting her again. Her power with him was gone for ever.

This is, of course, only what he thinks he feels, but we do not discover that he has changed until Anne herself finds out from his love letter.

The crushing phrase 'Her power with him was gone for ever' is particularly poignant as it is placed at the end of a chapter in which the reader has been privy to all Anne's fluctuations of feeling as the inevitable meeting with Wentworth approaches and takes place. Shifting the point of view from that of the narrator to that of Anne herself Jane Austen shows how obsessed her heroine is with Wentworth, though it never shows in her behaviour, and how ceaselessly she speculates about his feelings, trying to suppress a flicker of hope that he may still have some interest in her. She begins very rationally:

> She would have liked to know how he felt as to a meeting. Perhaps indifferent, if indifference could exist under such circumstances. He must be either indifferent or unwilling. Had he wished ever to see her again, he need not have waited till this time; he would have done what she could not but believe that in his place she should have done long ago. (Chapter 7)

When Charles and Mary meet him they find him reluctant to call at the Cottage: 'Anne understood it. He wished to avoid seeing her.' After she has met him herself she can no longer be so sensible:

> Alas! with all her reasonings, she found, that to retentive feelings eight years may be little more than nothing.
> Now, how were his sentiments to be read? Was this like wishing to avoid her? And the next moment she was hating herself for the folly which asked the question. (Chapter 7)

From the end of Chapter 7 onwards the reader can only speculate with Anne about Captain Wentworth's feelings; this means that the reader also pays close attention to details of behaviour and examines casual phrases for significance as he would if he were in a comparable situation in life. When Captain Wentworth sees to it that Anne is given a ride home in Admiral Croft's gig after the walk in Chapter 10 we wonder, as Anne does, what motivates him:

> She understood him. He could not forgive her,—but he could not be unfeeling . . . It was a remainder of former sentiment; it was an impulse of pure, though unacknowledged friendship; it was a proof of his own warm and amiable heart, which she could not contemplate without emotions so compounded of pleasure and pain, that she knew not which prevailed.

Jane Austen fills another trivial incident with meaning by her use of point of view in Chapter 9, when Captain Wentworth releases Anne from little Walter's clutches. We are permitted only to experience the scene as Anne herself experiences it. She is already intensely embarrassed by being accidentally left with Charles Hayter and Captain Wentworth, of whom Charles Hayter is jealous. She conceals her feeling by kneeling beside her sick nephew, Charles, but his brother Walter climbs on her back and refuses to get off:

She found herself in the state of being released from him; some one was taking him from her, though he bent down her head so much, that his sturdy little hands were unfastened from around her neck, and he was resolutely borne away, before she knew that Captain Wentworth had done it.

Her sensations on the discovery made her perfectly speechless. She could not even thank him.

Mr Elliot is as mysterious as Captain Wentworth; his creator gives us direct insight into his mind and again, given the same evidence, we agree and wonder with Anne. Here the narrator uses Anne's consciousness, not her own voice:

Mr Elliot was too generally agreeable. Various as were the tempers in her father's house, he pleased them all. He endured too well,—stood too well with everybody. (Chapter 17)

The novel depends for its success on this method; the two men remain a mystery and so the reader's interest both in them and in the minutiae of human behaviour is sustained. Actions are described but the motivation behind them is not; the 'seemed' in the following passage, when Anne meets Mr Ellliot for the first time, shows that the point of view is hers:

It was evident that the gentleman, (completely a gentleman in manner) admired her exceedingly. Captain Wentworth looked round at her instantly in a way which showed his noticing of it. He gave her a momentary glance,—a glance of brightness, which seemed to say, 'That man is struck with you.' (Chapter 12)

The reader only finds out for sure the changes that have been taking place in Captain Wentworth when he himself explains them to Anne:

He had imagined himself indifferent, when he had only been angry; and he had been unjust to her merits, because he had been a sufferer from them . . . He was obliged to acknowledge that only at Uppercross had he learnt to do her justice, and only at Lyme had he begun to understand himself. (Chapter 23)

We might ask why Jane Austen, as she depends so much on the reader's experiencing only what Anne experiences, did not use a first-person narration and make her heroine tell the story herself, as Jane Eyre does. The answer is suggested by the titles of the two novels; *Jane Eyre* is about its heroine, *Persuasion* is about the effect of social and personal pressure on several characters, particularly on Anne Elliot. Although *Persuasion* is a moving love story, Jane Austen wants her reader to maintain a certain detachment from it, and to be able to perceive the absurdity as well as the seriousness of romantic love. In a characteristic passage she shifts the reader abruptly from his involvement with Anne, as she realises how completely she loves Captain Wentworth, to a comment from the narrator which makes Anne seem an ordinary young woman in love:

> Be the conclusion of the present suspense good or bad, her affection would be his for ever. Their union, she believed, could not divide her more from other men, than their final separation.
> Prettier musings of high-wrought love and eternal constancy could never have passed along the streets of Bath than Anne was sporting with from Camden-place to Westgate-buildings. It was almost enough to spread purification and perfume all the way. (Chapter 21)

The narrative method in such a passage makes the reader aware of part of the meaning of the book; he is constantly shown characters engrossed in their own affairs. When she arrives at Uppercross Anne wishes 'that other Elliots could have her advantage in seeing how unknown, or unconsidered there, were the affairs which at Kellynch Hall were treated as of such general publicity and pervading interest' (Chapter 6). She feels that 'another lesson, in the art of knowing our own nothingness beyond our own circle, was become necessary for her' (Chapter 6). But the author makes clear through her narrative method that even as sensitive a character as Anne is self-obsessed, and she involves the reader in the self-obsession. As Anne and Lady Russell approach Captain Wentworth in Bath we see from Anne's point of view:

> She could thoroughly comprehend the sort of fascination he must possess over Lady Russell's mind, the difficulty it must be for her to withdraw her eyes, the astonishment she must be feeling that eight or nine years should have passed over him, and in foreign climes and in active service too, without robbing him of one personal grace! (Chapter 19)

When we discover that Lady Russell has only been peering out of the window to look for some special curtains, we can share in Anne's mortification, and, at the same time, understand that what is of vital importance to one man may be seen quite differently by another. Everyone must have his own concerns but needs the perspective on them that is provided by others.

Jane Austen also needs the narrator's voice to balance Anne's, because Anne is too gentle to allow herself to express the kind of insight that the narrator has into some of the characters and situations in the novel. The acid comparison of Sir Walter to a valet in the first chapter sets a tone characteristic of the narrator though not of Anne:

Few women could think more of their personal appearance than he did; nor could the valet of any new made lord be more delighted with the place he held in society. He considered the blessing of beauty as inferior only to the blessing of a baronetcy; and the Sir Walter Elliot, who united these gifts, was the constant object of his warmest respect and devotion.

The narrator is almost as sharp with other characters which heightens the reader's respect for those her wit spares. In conversation with Mrs Musgrove, Mrs Croft assures her that Bermuda and Bahama are not called the West Indies:

Mrs Musgrove had not a word to say in dissent; she could not accuse herself of having ever called them any thing in the whole course of her life. (Chapter 8)

Elizabeth is similarly ridiculed:

Elizabeth was, for a short time, suffering a good deal. . . . It was a struggle between propriety and vanity; but vanity got the better, and then Elizabeth was happy again. (Chapter 22)

Anne, unlike Elizabeth Bennet in *Pride and Prejudice*, would not express herself with such witty savagery if she could; the tension between Anne's point of view and the narrator's provides the reader with sympathetic insight into the central situation and a distanced perception of it.

Physical description

Scott wrote about Jane Austen's 'truth of description' and Charlotte Brontë of her 'elegant but confined houses'; in the light of these comment a reader might assume that realistically detailed physical description of places and people would be a crucial part of her method. But, though the reader has impressions of what characters and their houses look like, it is difficult to locate where they come from in the novel. Elizabeth is 'handsome', Anne has 'delicate features and mild dark eyes' (Chapter 1) which are very different from Sir Walter's, Captain Wentworth is glowing and manly. All these are vague descriptions compared with those in the first chapter of a much less realistic novel, *Jane Eyre*, where we are told that John Reed had 'a dingy and unwholesome skin' and 'a dim and bleared eye and flabby cheeks'. We know about Mrs Clay's freckles and Admiral Croft's complexion because they matter to Sir Walter but the narrator gives us no such details. Mr Elliot is 'not handsome' but has 'an agreeable person' (Chapter 12); Captain Harville is tall and dark 'with a sensible, benevolent countenance' and

Captain Benwick has 'a pleasing face and a melancholy air, just as he ought to have' (Chapter 11). All these descriptions allow almost total licence to the reader's imagination as such adjectives as 'sensible' and 'pleasing' are far from being visually precise.

The same is true of descriptions of place, with the one exception of Lyme. The reader is told that the Cottage has been modernised and has a verandah and french windows, and that the house in Bath has two large drawing rooms; there are passing references in the dialogue to pieces of furniture but the reader finds out little compared with what Charlotte Brontë would tell him. Such detail as there is, is there to illustrate character rather than to depict the scene for its own sake:

> They all went indoors with their new friends, and found rooms so small as none but those who invite from the heart could think capable of accommodating so many. (Chapter 11)

Anne is susceptible to melancholy:

> Her *pleasure* in the walk must arise from the exercise and the day, from the view of the last smiles of the year upon the tawny leaves and withered hedges, and from repeating to herself some few of the thousand poetical descriptions extant of autumn. (Chapter 10)

The description that follows this passage seems not to be there for its own sake but to put the reader on his guard against excessive poetical sentiment:

> The ploughs at work, and the fresh-made path spoke the farmer, counteracting the sweets of poetical despondence, and meaning to have spring again.

Jane Austen commented on a niece's novel: 'You describe a sweet place, but your descriptions are often more minute than will be liked. You give too many particulars of right hand & left'.* She does not explain her criticism but is clearly aware of the lack of detail in her own descriptions. The fact that most readers have a clear impression of what the characters and their houses look like is related to Jane Austen's understanding of her own kind of realism. What she says to her reader by implication through her lack of physical detail is: 'You know the kind of man/place I am describing; you have met him/been there.' In a curious way the lack of detail in the novel establishes an intimacy between the author and reader which the Victorian habit of addressing the 'dear reader' lacks; Jane Austen assumes that we know what baronets, manly naval officers and an 'elegant little woman of seven and twenty' (Chapter 17) are like and she allows us to picture them as

Letters, 9 September 1814, p.401

we please. Lyme Regis, and to a lesser extent Bath, are actual places which the reader may not have visited, so she fills the picture in more fully there. The description of Mr Rochester in *Jane Eyre* is more dogmatic; we are required to believe that his swarthy and grim features are sexually attractive, though this may not chime with our own experience. Because we can imagine Jane Austen's characters and places as we like we have the illusion that when we read about them we are reading about people in the real world; it heightens the realistic sense of life in the novel.

Plot

The plot of *Persuasion* is a complex fusion of the realistic and the non-realistic. It is possible to argue that it has the appeal of a fairy-story. Anne is in a way a Cinderella figure whose charms few people recognise, and she has a wicked father and two morally ugly sisters. The facts that she gradually emerges from obscurity, is recognised as beautiful, and is reunited with the handsome prince are both realistically credible and satisfying in terms of the reader's fantasy.

However, the means of reuniting the two central characters is prosaic compared with the separation and reunion of Mr Rochester and Jane Eyre. *Persuasion* is as uneventful as Jane Austen's own life; it is only because we are made to feel their significance for Anne that we can interest ourselves in such events as an aunt being freed from the grip of a naughty little nephew, or a party of people taking a country walk. The very uneventfulness of everyday life is commented on when something a little more dramatic than usual does happen and Louisa falls. Because the reader is involved in the feelings of the characters he participates in the consternation caused:

> He put out his hands; she was too precipitate by half a second, she fell on the pavement on the Lower Cobb, and was taken up lifeless!
> There was no wound, no blood, no visible bruise; but her eyes were closed, she breathed not, her face was like death.—The horror of that moment to all who stood around! (Chapter 12)

Jane Austen, however, almost immediately reduces the tension of the moment by showing other people's reactions to it:

> Many were collected near them, to be useful if wanted, at any rate, to enjoy the sight of a dead young lady, nay, two dead young ladies, for it proved twice as fine as the first report.

Here she mocks the universal human appetite for news and excitement, and throughout the novel the narrative interest is sustained by commonplace and not extraordinary events. Both *Pride and Prejudice* and

Mansfield Park culminate in unexpected elopements but *Persuasion* is more restricted in its action. Louisa's fall does cause anxiety but it is the kind of domestic upheaval that the reader is probably familiar with, and is of no interest to others though it is so momentous to those involved, which is also a situation that the reader may recognise. Anne finds she has been engrossed by it when she meets Lady Russell:

> She was actually forced to exert herself, to meet Lady Russell with anything like the appearance of equal solicitude, on topics which had by nature the first claim on her. (Chapter 13)

Even in *Emma* there is a mystery surrounding Jane Fairfax which is sustained throughout the novel and stimulates the reader's curiosity. *Persuasion* is the only one of her novels in which Jane Austen completely excludes manipulating the reader's interest through dramatic events, and relies on her ability to imbue commonplace happenings with moral and emotional significance.

Character

Method of characterisation

Jane Austen focuses the central preoccupation of her fiction by the way in which she introduces her characters to us; we generally meet their moral qualities first:

> Vanity was the beginning and the end of Sir Walter Elliot's character; vanity of person and of situation. (Chapter 1)

> She was a benevolent, charitable, good woman, and capable of strong attachments; most correct in her conduct, strict in her notions of decorum, and with manners that were held a standard of good-breeding. (of Lady Russell, Chapter 2)

> Mary had not Anne's understanding or temper. While well, and happy, and properly attended to, she had great good humour and excellent spirits; but any indisposition sunk her completely; she had no resources for solitude; and inheriting a considerable share of the Elliot self-importance, was very prone to add to every distress that of fancying herself neglected and ill-used. (Chapter 5)

D.H. Lawrence (1885-1930) wrote a hundred years later 'Never trust the teller, trust the tale' and Charles Dickens (1812-70) gave much the same advice in a letter about writing novels to Mrs Gaskell (1810-65); it is curious that an artist as conscious of the fineness of her 'little bit of ivory' should state her characters' moral qualities so deliberately. Both Lawrence and Dickens think that moral character should emerge from the way in which fictional people behave in the novel; that the novelist should avoid direct comment on his characters and allow the reader to interpret the action for himself, with the guidance provided by the language with which the author creates the character. Jane Austen could have done this; we could not mistake Sir Walter's vanity when we hear him discussing whom he is prepared to be seen with in public. The fact that she does not always introduce her characters by a summary of their moral qualities suggests that she uses the narrator's statement about the characters to achieve a particular response from the reader.

She is completely confident as the narrator in her moral judgements and she is interested in the morality rather than the psychology of her characters. Her method of introducing such characters as Sir Walter encourages us to think of him as we think of casual acquaintances in life, defined by his predominant characteristic. The novel is full of words connected with judgement and justice; there is no exploration of what makes Sir Walter vain so we are not invited to extend any sympathy to him, as we are to George Eliot's apparently unappealing characters such as Mr Casaubon or Mr Bulstrode, in *Middlemarch*. The reader is invited to acquiesce in the narrator's moral judgement through the placing of the generalising comment; immediately after the introductory passage on Mary there is a dialogue between Mary and Anne:

'So, you are come at last! I began to think I should never see you. I am so ill I can hardly speak. I have not seen a creature the whole morning!'

'I am sorry to find you unwell,' replied Anne. 'You sent me such a good account of yourself on Thursday!'

'Yes, I made the best of it; I always do; but I was very far from well at the time; and I do not think I ever was so ill in my life as I have been all this morning.' (Chapter 5)

The reader recognises what kind of woman Mary is and judges her; the fact that her mother died when she was quite young is never suggested as an extenuating circumstance to explain her lack of self-discipline as it might be in a later or more psychological novelist.

The authority of the moral judgements made by the narrator could make the novel unsympathetic to the modern reader who lives in a world where moral judgements are normally much less absolute. Jane Austen avoids pomposity by her ironic wit:

Sir Walter, like a good father (having met with one or two private disappointments in very unreasonable applications), prided himself on remaining single for his dear daughters' sake. For one daughter, his eldest, he would really have given up any thing, which he had not been very much tempted to do. (Chapter 1)

The reader needs to collaborate with the writer to perceive irony, and in so doing enjoys his own sense of superiority which the narrator says we all have:

> Anne always contemplated them as some of the happiest creatures of her acquaintance; but still, saved as we all are by some comfortable feeling of superiority from wishing for the possibility of exchange, she would not have given up her own more elegant and cultivated mind for all their enjoyments. (Chapter 5)

Nevertheless there is a pervasive moral discrimination between characters in the novel made by the narrator and by the characters themselves, and expected of the reader:

> 'Fanny Harville was a very superior creature; and his attachment to her was indeed attachment. A man does not recover from such a devotion of the heart to such a woman!—He ought not—he does not.' (Chapter 20)

> He had not understood the perfect excellence of the mind with which Louisa's could so ill bear a comparison; or the perfect, unrivalled hold it possessed over his own. There, he had learnt to distinguish between the steadiness of principle and the obstinacy of self-will, between the darings of heedlessness and the resolution of a collected mind. (Chapter 23)

This is heightened by the way in which characters are placed in parallel situations: both Captain Benwick and Captain Wentworth have lost the women they loved, Mr Musgrove and Sir Walter are both the fathers of marriageable daughters, Mary and Mrs Harville both have small children, Mr Elliot and Captain Wentworth both love Anne, Anne and Louisa both become engaged in the course of the novel.

Anne

Anne is an unusual heroine for Jane Austen in several respects. She wrote to her niece, Fanny, about heroines in novels saying: 'Pictures of perfection as you know make me sick & wicked.' In the same letter she refers to Anne Elliot: 'You may *perhaps* like the Heroine, as she is almost too good for me.'* Anne is very close to being a picture of perfection and yet she remains sympathetic and credible. This is partly because the reader knows a good deal of what is happening in her head though she rarely betrays her feelings, and we know that she constantly has small hopes and expectations which are disappointed:

*Letters, 23 March 1817, p.487

> The usual fate of Anne attended her, in having something very opposite from her inclinations fixed on. She disliked Bath, and did not think it agreed with her—and Bath was to be her home. (Chapter 2)

We come very quickly to trust Anne's judgement of character and have in many cases to depend on it as the narrator gives us no extra guidance. Our first experience of Anne's moral discernment comes through the discussion of Sir Walter's debts:

> She considered it an act of indispensable duty to clear away the claims of creditors, with all the expedition which the most comprehensive retrenchments could secure, and saw no dignity in any thing short of it. She wanted it to be prescribed and felt as a duty. (Chapter 2)

This perception and many others lead us to trust her on questions which we cannot resolve for ourselves:

> She could not but think, as far as she might judge from memory and experience, that Captain Wentworth was not in love with either. They were in love with him; yet there it was not love. It was a little fever of admiration; but it might, probably must, end in love with some. (Chapter 10)

Apart from being so perfect a heroine, Anne Elliot is unusual among Jane Austen's heroines in being a mature woman. The publisher's blurb of the Penguin edition claims that Anne's reunion with Captain Wentworth 'forces a recognition of the false values that drove them apart' and this implies that Anne is a conventional heroine in that we see her growing to self-knowledge, as we see Elizabeth Bennet, Catherine Morland and Emma doing. This is a misreading of the novel, for Anne at the end says she believes she was right to take Lady Russell's advice:

> 'I must believe that I was right, much as I suffered from it, that I was perfectly right in being guided by the friend whom you will love better than you do now. To me, she was in the place of a parent. Do not mistake me, however. I am not saying that she did not err in her advice.' (Chapter 23)

She does not blame Lady Russell for her advice but learns that there are subjects on which they do not agree, 'she and her excellent friend could sometimes think differently', and so it does not surprise her 'that Lady Russell should see nothing suspicious or inconsistent . . . in Mr Elliot's great desire of a reconciliation' (Chapter 16). Anne is remarkable from the beginning for the maturity of her judgement; she gives up Captain Wentworth in the 'belief of being prudent, and self-denying principally for *his* advantage' (Chapter 4). She is in fact superior to Lady Russell in this respect:

> There is a quickness of perception in some, a nicety in the discernment of character, a natural penetration, in short, which no experience in others can equal, and Lady Russell had been less gifted in this part of understanding than her young friend. (Chapter 24)

Her awareness of the areas of disagreement between herself and Lady Russell is the main difference between Anne as a young girl and as 'an elegant little woman of seven and twenty'.

Her elegance is stressed; Mr and Mrs Musgrove are 'not at all elegant' but Anne has 'an elegant and cultivated mind' (Chapter 5), while Elizabeth only has 'well-bred, elegant manners' (Chapter 15) and shares her father's 'heartless elegance' (Chapter 22). Anne is presented as the best representative of her type, a daughter of the landed gentry. Elizabeth's elegant manners are for display; when she has to struggle between 'propriety and vanity' vanity wins. Mary has not even elegant manners but is vulgar in her Elliot pride.

One of the ways in which Jane Austen prevents her 'picture of perfection' from making the reader 'sick and wicked' is by occasionally allowing him to laugh at her. She is presented as being slightly absurdly sentimental, inclined to quote sonnets 'fraught with the apt analogy of the declining year, with declining happiness, and the images of youth and hope, and spring, all gone together'. (Chapter 10) She is nostalgic about an event the minute it is over; she looks 'back, with fond regret, to the bustles of Uppercross and the seclusion of Kellynch' (Chapter 14) the day she leaves for Bath. She is occasionally naïve in her moral judgements; when she tries to assess the character of Mr Elliot she equates his lack of seriousness with the observation that 'Sunday-travelling had been a common thing' (Chapter 17). Even for an early nineteenth-century audience, travelling on a Sunday must have seemed a peccadillo for a man whom they may already suspect to be 'black at heart, hollow and black' (Chapter 21). When Anne is beginning to be happy in her love for Captain Wentworth she is, like most lovers, both touching and absurd in her pretty 'musings of high-wrought love and eternal constancy' (Chapter 21).

Sir Walter

Even when she laughs at her heroine Jane Austen never allows the reader to lose sight of her delicacy and real refinement. Sir Walter's ostentatious fastidiousness is a cloak for snobbery and selfishness whereas Anne has sensitive discrimination in her dealings with others. Sir Walter is horrified when he discovers that Anne visits 'a Mrs Smith', 'a mere Mrs Smith, an every day Mrs Smith, of all people and all names in the world' (Chapter 17). Sir Walter is the opposite of Anne; he has all the appurtenances of refinement, but is actually vulgar in his obsession with his own appearance and importance. He shows no awareness that his comfortable way of life has recently been menaced by the Napoleonic Wars; Admiral Croft fought at Trafalgar but that does not improve Sir Walter's opinion of him or of naval men generally because the navy raises 'men to honours which their fathers and grandfathers never dreamt of' and because 'a sailor grows old sooner than any other man' (Chapter 3). There is a rich irony in all this, as Sir Walter's way of life is exposed in the novel as being singularly self-centred and purposeless. He has no sense of duty towards his tenants, and that they have no respect for him is suggested by the wry account of his departure from Kellynch, when he prepared himself 'with condescending bows for all the afflicted tenantry and cottagers who might have had a hint to shew themselves' (Chapter 5). The fact that Sir Walter lives for pleasure and the gratification of his vanity is made clear when the reader is invited to compare him with Admiral Croft, his tenant and a man who has earned his social position by his bravery. He tells Anne that he has moved all the large mirrors out of his dressing-room and says of her father, 'I should think he must be rather a dressy man for his time of life' (Chapter 13). The Admiral's dignity provides an implicit comment on Sir Walter throughout the novel; Sir Walter hesitates to introduce the Admiral to Lady Dalrymple but does 'think and talk a great deal more about the Admiral, than the Admiral ever thought or talked about him' (Chapter 18). Sir Walter forces his distant cousin Lady Dalrymple to acknowledge their relationship, together with her daughter, Miss Carteret, who is 'so plain and so awkward, that she would never have been tolerated in Camden-place but for her birth' (Chapter 16). This makes Sir Walter even more grotesque, as he is at once servile and affected:

> 'Lady Dalrymple, Lady Dalrymple,' was the rejoicing sound; and with all the eagerness compatible with anxious elegance, Sir Walter and his two ladies stepped forward to meet her. (Chapter 20)

Sir Walter's situation is also compared with Mr Musgrove's; just as Captain Wentworth is Anne's social inferior, so Charles Hayter is Henrietta's, but is given her hand in marriage by Mr Musgrove. Anne comments to Charles Musgrove: 'Your father and mother seem so totally free from all those ambitious feelings which have led to so much misconduct and misery' (Chapter 22). Sir Walter's response to Anne's marriage characteristically involves his vanity: he comes to think Captain Wentworth very handsome and 'all this, assisted by his well-sounding name, enabled Sir Walter at last' (Chapter 24) to inscribe their marriage in his copy of the Baronetage.

Persuasion is in many respects a more sombre novel than Jane Austen's earlier ones; the treatment of Sir Walter contributes towards this. The novel opens with him and not with Anne, and in the final chapter he is the same vain self-centred baronet whose life is spent in 'nothing-saying' (Chapter 20). In this he differs radically from other foolish fathers of heroines in the novels, Sir Thomas in *Mansfield Park* and Mr Bennet in *Pride and Prejudice*. Both these fathers are made to suffer and feel remorse, Mr Bennet for his laxity as a father and Sir Thomas for his excessive severity. The reader wants Sir Walter to suffer because he cannot see Anne's worth but there is no transformation, and it is Anne who suffers 'as lively pain as her mind could well be sensible of' because she has nothing to offer Captain Wentworth in her family 'of respectability, of harmony, of good-will' (Chapter 24).

Captain Wentworth and Mr Elliot

Captain Wentworth and Mr Elliot are characterised differently from the other characters, because of their relationship with Anne. The only mystery in this novel, unlike Jane Austen's other novels, is one of character; the reader asks himself constantly as he reads 'what does Captain Wentworth feel about Anne now?' and 'what is Mr Elliot's real feeling about his cousins and uncle?' Apart from a brief account, at the end of the seventh chapter, of Captain Wentworth's feelings about Anne when he first meets her again after their separation, we can only speculate with Anne about any change that may be taking place in him, and try to interpret his words and actions, until his declaration of love at the end. Similarly we know nothing but what we can deduce through Anne's observation of Mr Elliot's sincerity or lack of it; he 'was rational, discreet, polished,—but he was not open . . .. This, to Anne, was a decided imperfection' (Chapter 17). Only at the end is the reader able to make sense of his character, with Anne, as a result of Mrs Smith's reveletations.

Both men are mentioned early in the novel; the reader's interest is stirred and then heightened by the way in which they first appear. Mr Elliot is initially sympathetic because he perceives immediately what the reader feels, that Anne is more appealing than Louisa and Henrietta, though as yet he is only a handsome stranger; this happens in Lyme and he looks at her 'with a degree of earnest admiration' (Chapter 12). The reader is given a series of reports of the impact that Captain Wentworth has made on the Musgroves before he appears; Louisa and Henrietta say 'how much handsomer, how infinitely more agreeable' he is than any other man they know:

> How glad they had been to hear papa invite him to stay to dinner—
> how sorry when he said it was quite out of his power—and how glad,
> again, when he had promised . . . to come and dine with them on the
> morrow, actually on the morrow! (Chapter 7)

This passage is characteristic of the compression of Jane Austen's
method of presenting character. She at once stimulates the reader's
interest in Captain Wentworth and tells him something about the
Musgrove girls without commenting on them directly. She shifts the
point of view from that of the narrator to that of the two pretty, silly
girls, and indicates to us, without using direct speech, how excitable
and effusive they are by the use of dashes and exclamation marks to
convey breathless chatter. We see the characters caught in the nexus of
social relationships which make up ordinary life, and we know people's
opinions about each other even though such opinions do not directly
further the plot. Henrietta looks upon Lady Russell 'as able to persuade
a person to any thing! I am afraid of her . . . because she is so very clever;
but I respect her amazingly.' (Chapter 12)

Characters as part of their group

We also see the characters as part of their group; Mary thinks that
Charles Hayter should not aspire to marry a Musgrove because he
comes from a poor family and the Musgroves now have a baronet's
daughter among them; her 'And, pray, who is Charles Hayter?' antici-
pates Sir Walter's strictures on Mrs Smith. Because Sir Walter and
Elizabeth wish to be part of the aristocratic group they will not risk
introducing the Crofts to Lady Dalrymple. Anne, an unrepresentative
member of her group, is outspoken about the meaninglessness of the
social groups that are so important to the rest of her family:

> Anne was ashamed. Had Lady Dalrymple and her daughter even
> been very agreeable, she would still have been ashamed of the agita-
> tion they created, but they were nothing . . .. 'My idea of good com-
> pany, Mr Elliot, is the company of clever, well-informed people.'
> (Chapter 16)

The most attractive group in the novel, because its bonds are those of a
common interest and not of rank, is the naval group. The words used
recurrently of Captain Wentworth, such as 'open', 'frank' and 'warm'
are also used of the other naval officers, and of their wives. Their conversation is lively and informal, and the women are as vigorous as their
men-folk. The juxtaposition of the leisured gentry and the active naval
officers is made explicit in Anne's comparison between Mr Elliot's
genteel manner and Captain Wentworth's impetuosity: 'she felt that

she could so much more depend upon the sincerity of those who sometimes looked or said a careless or a hasty thing, than of those whose
presence of mind never varied, whose tongue never slipped' (Chapter
17). Captain Wentworth is consistently described as 'glowing' and
'manly', and in this he is representative of the values of his group and as
far as possible from Sir Walter who has no masculine protectiveness
towards his daughters or his dependants.

The Musgroves constitute a separate group, which defines by contrast the values of both the gentry and the naval officers and their wives.
They are not snobbish, and in some respects resemble the naval group
in their warmth and hospitality; Jane Austen uses an unusual amount
of descriptive detail in the following passage to convey the warmth of
their family life:

> On one side was a table, occupied by some chattering girls, cutting
> up silk and gold paper; and on the other were tressels and trays,
> bending under the weight of brawn and cold pies, where riotous boys
> were holding high revel; the whole completed by a roaring Christmas
> fire, which seemed determined to be heard, in spite of all the noise of
> the others . . .. Mr Musgrove made a point of paying his respects to
> Lady Russell, and sat down close to her for ten minutes, talking with
> a very raised voice, but, from the clamour of the children on his
> knees, generally in vain. It was a fine family-piece. (Chapter 14)

Yet they are also criticised. Charles 'did nothing with much zeal, but
sport; and his time was otherwise trifled away, without benefit from
books, or any thing else' (Chapter 6). His sisters' 'modern minds and
manners' (Chapter 5) are commented on indirectly by Admiral Croft:
'And very nice young ladies they both are; I hardly know one from the
other' (Chapter 10). No such mistake could be made about the Elliot
sisters, and both Louisa and Henrietta have what is presented as an
almost culpable adaptability. Charles is mystified by the change in
Louisa: 'She is altered: there is no running or jumping about, no laugh-
ing or dancing; it is quite different' (Chapter 22).

In the depiction of individuals and groups moral qualities predomin-
ate but they may be presented to us directly by the narrator, as with Sir
Walter, or indirectly so that we have, until the end of the novel, to form
opinions from a character's behaviour and the effect he has on others,
as with Mr Elliot. Jane Austen can suggest moral qualities with the
utmost economy by the repetition of significant words and by the
grammatical structure of her sentences and their place on the page. The
two-year-old Walter's sturdy obstinacy in the incident when he is told
to leave his aunt alone is suggested in a one-sentence paragraph, and the
inversion of the normal word-order. 'But not a bit did Walter stir'
(Chapter 9).

Language

At the time when Jane Austen was writing *Persuasion* she was already unwell with a disease that was to prove fatal. Though her sister Cassandra destroyed most of her letters on serious personal subjects two survive which reflect her feelings about death. She writes to her nephew hoping that he will possess, if he is ever ill, loving friends to nurse him and 'the greatest blessing of all, in the consciousness of not being unworthy of their Love. *I* could not feel this.'* The letter ends there, in its abruptness suggesting painful remorse. A letter written a few days earlier, when she thought she was recovering, ends in a prayer: 'God has restored me—& may I be more fit to appear before him when I *am* summoned, than I should have been now!'†

The two letters combine to convey an impression that their author is not simply repeating pious platitudes but feels and fears her own spiritual inadequacies, and believes in divine justice. A similar concern with moral discrimination and judgement is to be found in *Persuasion*, and the words which recur most frequently are such abstract nouns as 'judgement', 'justice', 'duty', 'principle' and 'character'. Anne's constant struggle is to control her feelings, another word which is often used, and to reconcile feeling with what she perceives to be duty. When Elizabeth and Sir Walter abuse Mrs Smith as a middle-aged woman with a common name, Anne thinks of Mrs Clay and longs to say something 'in defence of *her* friend's not very dissimilar claims to theirs, but her sense of personal respect to her father prevented her' (Chapter 17).

This almost legal strain in the language ('in defence of', 'claims') is characteristic of the novel; in the following passage Anne brings Mr Elliot to trial in her mind. The words connected with moral and legal judgement and moral discrimination are in italic:

> And it was not only that her feelings were adverse to any man save one; her *judgement*, on a serious *consideration* of the possibilities of such a *case*, was against Mr Elliot.
>   Though they had now been acquainted a month, she could not be satisfied that she really knew his *character*. That he was a *sensible* man, an *agreeable* man,—that he talked well, professed good *opinions*, seemed to *judge* properly and as a *man of principle*,—this was all clear enough. He certainly knew what was *right*, nor could she fix on any one *article* of *moral duty* evidently *transgressed*; but yet she would have been afraid to answer for his *conduct*. (Chapter 17)

Anne and the narrator constantly invite the reader to make judgements about the characters, though none of them does anything as clearly

Letters, 27 May 1817, p.497
†*Letters*, 22 May 1817, p.495

immoral as Henry Crawford or Mr Wickham do in other novels.

The novel is about persuasion and the word recurs frequently; Anne was persuaded not to marry Captain Wentworth by Lady Russell. Experience has changed her view; 'she was persuaded . . . she should yet have been a happier woman in maintaining the engagement, than she had been in the sacrifice of it' (Chapter 4). The word 'sacrifice' has spiritual connotations; the word 'persuaded' suggests a fusion of many of the qualities in the novel as the process of persuasion Anne was subjected to was the tempering of feeling by reason. Though Captain Wentworth thought her sacrifice 'the effect of over-persuasion' (Chapter 7) Anne is often 'unpersuadable' (Chapter 7); she will not be persuaded by Lady Russell to consider Mr Elliot as a husband, though she shudders at the thought that 'it was just possible that she might have been persuaded' (Chapter 21) by her. She is concerned about the 'unfortunate persuasion' of Captain Wentworth's that she intends to marry Mr Elliot.

Susceptibility to persuasion is one of the moral qualities that is examined in the novel. Captain Wentworth's view is attractively decisive:

'It is the worst evil of too yielding and indecisive a character, that no influence over it can be depended on.—You are never sure of a good impression being durable. Every body may sway it; let those who would be happy be firm.' (Chapter 10)

When the determined Louisa has fallen as a result of her obstinacy the reader is invited, through Anne, to wonder about persuadability as a virtue:

Anne wondered whether it ever occurred to him now, to question the justness of his own previous opinion as to the universal felicity and advantage of firmness of character; and whether it might not strike him, that, like all other qualities of the mind, it should have its proportions and limits. She thought it could scarcely escape him to feel, that a persuadable temper might sometimes be as much in favour of happiness, as a very resolute character. (Chapter 12)

Proportions, limits and context have to be considered in relation to persuasion; the irony here is that the 'firm' Louisa is persuaded, by proximity, to fall in love with Captain Benwick and forget Captain Wentworth, which the 'indecisive' Anne cannot do. Anne, who has learnt so many lessons in how to discriminate, comments indirectly on Louisa's persuadability when she explains to Captain Wentworth why he was wrong to fear that she was in love with Mr Elliot: 'If I was wrong in yielding to persuasion once, remember that it was to persuasion exerted on the side of safety, not of risk. When I yielded, I thought it was to duty; but no duty could be called in aid here. In marrying a man indifferent to me, all risk would have been incurred, and all duty violated' (Chapter 23).

When a reader remembers *Wuthering Heights* he remembers, among other aspects of the novel, plenty of things: windows, dogs, cloaks, fires, flowers, keys and feathers. There are few 'things' in *Persuasion* and those there are mostly exist only to illustrate character, such as Sir Walter's mirrors and Admiral Croft's horror of them. Even the glossy hazel-nut that Captain Wentworth picks up on his walk with Louisa becomes an explicit symbol of a moral quality: the language constantly requires that the reader should discriminate, evaluate and judge. The final chapter of the novel is characteristic of the whole; Anne and Captain Wentworth are compared with ordinary young people in love, and are shown to have a moral right to their happiness:

> This may be bad morality to conclude with, but I believe it to be truth; and if such parties succeed, how should a Captain Wentworth and an Anne Elliot, with the advantage of maturity of mind, conscious-ess of right, and one independent fortune between them, fail of bear-ing down every opposition?

Themes

The central theme of the novel has already been discussed. Unlike *Persuasion*, other novels by Jane Austen contain fairy tale elements; Fanny Price in *Mansfield Park* is a Cinderella figure, and Emma in *Emma* a Sleeping Beauty, while in *Pride and Prejudice* Mr Darcy is a beast who becomes a handsome prince. *Persuasion* is a mature love story and is peculiar in being so: Anne 'had been forced into prudence in her youth, she learned romance as she grew older—the natural sequel of an unnatural beginning' (Chapter 4). Neither central character changes radically or gains self-knowledge as they already have it; both come to a gradual recognition of what they had known eight years earlier. They, and particularly Anne, have what is shown to be a rare ability to temper strong feeling with reason and refined moral awareness. The reader is given a privileged sense of sharing in the sensitivity of Anne's responses to what happens to her. He may also recognise from his own experience that it is often the apparently trivial incidents in one's life that are charged with the greatest personal significance: incidents such as Anne's release by Captain Wentworth from little Walter, or Captain Wentworth's asking Anne to stay in Lyme to nurse Louisa.

Beside the personal theme and inextricably bound up with it there is a wider social theme. It is not just twentieth-century society that changes fast; in her Advertisement for *Northanger Abbey* Jane Austen apologises that it may be out of date as it was written thirteen years earlier and 'during that period, places, manners, books, and opinions have undergone considerable changes'. Throughout *Persuasion* there is recognition of such change. Mr Elliot is obliquely criticised for disrespect towards the Elliot family and is outraged: 'He, who had ever boasted of being an Elliot, and whose feelings, as to connection, were only too strict to suit the unfeudal tone of the present day!' (Chapter 15). There is a sense that the value of social rank is being questioned, though Sir Walter certainly does not question it.

It is because such characters as Elizabeth, Sir Walter and Mr Elliot accept unquestioningly the social superiority of the aristocracy and gentry and Anne disagrees with them that the reader may feel uneasy. Anne feels that Sir Walter has forfeited his right to Kellynch Hall: 'she could not but in conscience feel that they were gone who deserved not to stay, and that Kellynch Hall had passed into better hands than its owners'. (Chapter 13) This idea is sustained throughout the novel:

> She must sigh that her father should feel no degradation in his change; should see nothing to regret in the duties and dignity of the resident land-holder; should find so much to be vain of in the littlenesses of a town. (Chapter 15)

The idea that the duties and dignities of Sir Walter's position should be inherited seems to be in question; Anne is impatient of rank for its own sake and rejects Mr Elliot's maxim that 'rank is rank' and intrinsically valuable. She has her own definition of good company as being 'clever, well-informed people, who have a great deal of conversation' (Chapter 16). Such people are not to be found 'in the elegant stupidity' (Chapter 19) of the evening parties the fashionable people in Bath frequent. The scathing passage at the beginning of the final chapter focuses for the reader on the contrast between Captain Wentworth and Sir Walter: Captain Wentworth 'was now esteemed quite worthy to address the daughter of a foolish spendthrift baronet, who had not principle or sense enough to maintain himself in the situation in which Providence had placed him' whereas his prospective son-in-law is as 'as high in his profession as merit and activity could place him'. Anne regards her rank as totally insignificant; she feels she has 'no relations to bestow on him which a man of sense could value' (Chapter 24).

The defining contrast with the fashionable gentry in the novel is provided by the naval group. They, including the women, have all the qualities of energy, concern and sympathy that Sir Walter and the Dalrymples lack. Anne often sees the Crofts in Bath and is 'delighted to see the Admiral's hearty shake of the hand when he encountered an old friend, and observe their eagerness of conversation when occasionally forming into a little knot of the navy, Mrs Croft looking as intelligent and keen as any of the officers around her' (Chapter 18). All the members of the naval group are warm and unpretentious; Captain Harville has an 'unaffected, easy kindness of manner' which gives him 'the feelings of an older acquaintance than he really was' (Chapter 23). This is juxtaposed against Sir Walter's anxiety about whether it is proper to introduce the Crofts to Lady Dalrymple; Sir Walter is seen as sterile and useless compared with the men, whom he despises, who have recently helped to save their country from Napoleon. The novel ends with a description of the happiness of a baronet's daughter who has become, in Jane Austen's phrase, not a captain's but a sailor's wife: she 'gloried in being a sailor's wife, but she must pay the tax of quick alarm for belonging to that profession which is, if possible, more distinguished in its domestic virtues than in its national importance.'

The novel makes a powerful attack on the degeneracy of the old order; Mr Elliot, as the baronet's heir, is exposed as a ruthless material-ist in comparison with Captain Wentworth who expects, and wants, to earn his position in society. The Musgroves are somewhere between the gentry and the active naval men, 'in a state of alteration, perhaps of improvement' (Chapter 5). Charles does 'nothing with much zeal, but sport' and trifles his time away 'without benefit from books, or any thing else' while his sisters live only 'to be fashionable, happy, and merry' (Chapter 5). Charles, Henrietta and Louisa all choose their spouses through being thrown together with them by accident, unlike Anne and Captain Wentworth, and their empty-headed cheerfulness seems to be measured not only by the characters of Captain Wentworth and Anne but by such minor characters as Nurse Rooke. Mrs Smith, though she has been to a fashionable school, can do nothing to earn money when she needs it, and Mrs Rooke helps her by teaching her to knit and finding buyers for the things she makes.

> 'Hers is a line for seeing human nature; and she has a fund of good sense and observation which, as a companion, make her infinitely superior to thousands of those who having only received "the best education in the world", know nothing worth attending to.'
> (Chapter 17)

But, to use Jane Austen's word, Anne is the most 'superior' character in the novel, superior in sensitivity, sympathy, intelligence and under-standing. Any generalisation about Jane Austen's themes has to be qualified. While *Persuasion* does undoubtedly criticise the self-indulgent indolence of Sir Walter's class it also shows that it is the class that pro-duces the 'elegant little woman of seven and twenty' whose 'elegant and cultivated mind' is, to a large extent, the medium through which the reader interprets the situation in the novel. It is a novel in which moral judgement is required of the reader and it is Anne's refined discernment which enables him to make that judgement.

Hints for study

How to read a novel

Most novels appeal to the human love of stories. It is a pity to spoil the experience of reading a novel by trying to take notes the first time you read it when all you want to do is find out what happens next. It is a good idea to read the novel straight through once and jot down impressions at the end of it. These may concern the meaning of the book or may record the vivid impact that certain scenes have had on you, or you may simply want to ask questions. At the end of a first reading of *Persuasion* you might want to ask how such a commonplace story has managed to sustain your interest, or you might want to comment on the impact on the reader of such an apparently ordinary incident as the removal of little Walter by Captain Wentworth in Chapter 9.

You will want to take detailed notes when you read the novel for the second time; for the purpose of writing essays or taking examinations, it is best to do so under headings. It is worth giving some thought to the headings and you may want to list the same references under various headings. For example the sentence in Chapter 1: 'Vanity was the beginning and end of Sir Walter Elliot's character; vanity of person and of situation', might appear under such headings as 'Method of characterisation', under 'Language' and under 'Function of the narrator'.

The categories into which you could divide notes on *Persuasion* might be something like this:

(1) Characterisation

(*i*) METHOD: a summary of a character's moral qualities followed by action showing those qualities

(*ii*) IRONY: the way in which the reader's response to a character is controlled by ironic presentation

(*iii*) INTIMACY: whether the author gives us a deep insight into the character's mind and emotions and whether this varies from one character to another

(*iv*) APPEARANCE: whether character is suggested by physical appearance

(2) Language

(*i*) NATURE: is it abstract or concrete language, colloquial or rhetorical, formal or informal? And why is it?

(*ii*) RECURRENT WORDS: certain words, which may be quite ordinary ones, when they are repeated in a work of literature acquire significance through this repetition. As you notice words recurring single them out and list the pages on which they appear and you may find a thematic pattern emerges. In *Persuasion* such words as 'duty', 'judgement', 'justice', 'feelings' and the verb 'seemed' recur, and you will notice other words which gain significance through being repeated.

(3) Narrative method

(*i*) POINT OF VIEW: has the narrator complete omniscience or does she tell the story mostly through the consciousness of one character? Or does she remain outside all the characters?

(*ii*) NARRATOR: has the narrator a distinctive tone? In *Persuasion* the narrator is consistently ironic.

(4) Plot

(*i*) REALISM: are the events described in the novel extraordinary or commonplace?

(*ii*) COMPLEXITY: how complicated is the story? If it is simple how does the author sustain the reader's interest in it?

(*iii*) PARALLELS: are there incidents which can be compared and contrasted within the novel, for example, the engagements between Captain Benwick and Louisa, and Captain Wentworth and Anne; the roles played by fathers (Mr Musgrove and Sir Walter) and sisters (Mrs Croft and Elizabeth)?

(5) Physical description

(*i*) DETAIL: how much detail about clothes, houses and places is there in the novel?

(*ii*) FUNCTION: is it used primarily to create places and people that may be strange to the reader or to illuminate character? In *Persuasion*, for example, the movement from autumn to spring suggests a rejuvenation in Anne.

(6) Theme

(*i*) THE THEME: or overall meaning of the novel, usually emerges as you take notes and begin to observe recurrent words and patterns in the plot. It is also clarified by the reader's consideration of his own response to the novel; in *Persuasion*, although he feels for Anne, the reader is not swept along on a tide of heightened emotion but has constantly to question the motives of the characters and guess their feelings.

How to write an essay

With detailed notes it is possible to express your own view of the novel in relation to the question asked. In order to prepare for an examination you should anticipate likely areas for questioning. The three most obvious ones are suggested, with sample answers, below.

If you are allowed to have the text of the novel in the examination with you, you will benefit from having made detailed notes on it, because this will help you to find your way around the text quickly. Also, if you do have the text with you, it is best to substantiate any point you make with a *brief* quotation. Do not leave large quotations to do the work for you; comment on the quotation in the way that is suggested below. If you cannot take the text into the examination try to memorise significant phrases such as 'the elegant little woman of seven and twenty' or 'her judgement . . . was against Mr Elliot'; when you want to illustrate a point refer to an incident or scene, mentioning the chapter if you can remember it, without quoting directly.

The most obvious questions about *Persuasion* are raised at the beginning of Part 3, Commentary: is Jane Austen's restricted world 'more *real* than *true*' and is she one of 'the greatest painters of human character'? Three aspects of these large questions might be considered:

(1) is the 'little bit (two Inches wide) of Ivory on which I work with so fine a Brush', as Jane Austen says in a letter, too restricted to be of interest to us now?

(2) what does the depiction of such minor characters as Lady Russell and Mrs Clay contribute to the meaning of *Persuasion*?

(3) does the realistic presentation of *Persuasion* prevent the novel from encompassing emotional truth and deep feeling?

Suggested outline of answer to (1)

(*i*) *Introduction.* The general question of whether art is necessarily the better for having a broad scope could be discussed. To enjoy a novel we should have confidence that the writer knows all about the world he or she is creating. If the writer makes mistakes in the depiction of people or places which are obvious to us, the illusion we have that we are reading about people who actually exist is destroyed. Jane Austen's fictional world in *Persuasion* is consistent and does not stretch our credulity; its realistic uneventfulness allows us to concentrate on the subtle interaction between the characters.

(*ii*) The fact that the characters are recognisable as human beings, not just as types such as baronets and admirals, could be made next, using such examples as Sir Walter's conceited expectation that Admiral Croft will be welcomed in Bath as the tenant of Kellynch Hall rather than as a veteran of Trafalgar. The intractability of the characters also makes them recognisably life-like: Lady Russell is as mistaken about Mr Elliot as she was about Captain Wentworth.

(*iii*) The incidents are brought alive by the author's attention to detail and the reader is made to feel with the characters. The intense embarrassment that Anne feels when she is left alone in Mary's cottage with her two nephews, Charles Hayter and Captain Wentworth is reflected in Jane Austen's narrative method; the reader sees only what Anne sees: 'She found herself in a state of being released from him [little Walter]; some one was taking him from her' (Chapter 9).

(*iv*) The plot is restricted in the sense that it does not include extraordinary coincidences or exciting events. Jane Austen's ability to sustain the reader's interest without having recourse to an eventful story might be commented on here. You could compare the original ending of the novel with Chapters 23 and 24 and show how unsatisfactory the original ending is in terms of our expectations of the characters. The pleasure given by reading the turning-points in the plot is derived from the dual perspective in which we see them: we feel their significance for the characters but also see how insignificant they are for others. After Louisa's fall we are told that 'the report of the accident had spread among the workmen and boatmen about the Cobb, and many were collected near them, to be useful if wanted, at any rate, to enjoy the sight of a dead young lady, nay, two dead young ladies, for it proved twice as fine as the first report' (Chapter 12). The moving final reunion between Captain Wentworth and Anne takes place surrounded by 'sauntering politicians, bustling house-keepers, flirting girls' (Chapter 23).

(*v*) The extraordinary quality that is demanded of the reader of *Persuasion* is moral scrutiny. Through Anne the narrator examines the smallest word or gesture and conveys a sense that the most trivial act has significance; it is mainly on small insensitivities that we judge the characters, for example Lady Russell's failure to respond to the 'fine family-piece' (Chapter 14). The kind of perception required of the reader, to observe irony and make moral judgements, is the opposite of restricted; it may liberate him or her into a finer awareness of the minutiae of human behaviour, and the comedy this can provide.

Suggested outline of answer to (2)

(i) *Introduction.* Lady Russell and Mrs Clay can both be seen in the novel as individuals and as members of their group. Lady Russell is one of the social élite and Mrs Clay would like to be; Mrs Clay forms part of a sub-group with Mr Elliot, Sir Walter and Elizabeth in that she fawns on her social superiors in order to rise in the social scale.

(ii) The depiction of Lady Russell is like that of Sir Walter; a summary of her moral qualities is our first introduction to her:

> She was a benevolent, charitable, good woman, and capable of strong attachments, most correct in her conduct . . . but she had prejudices on the side of ancestry; she had a value for rank and consequence, which blinded her a little to the faults of those who possessed them. (Chapter 2)

We then see these qualities in action when she tries to persuade Sir Walter to retrench. Mrs Clay is introduced more briefly but in the same manner:

> She was a clever young woman, who understood the art of pleasing; the art of pleasing, at least, at Kellynch Hall. (Chapter 2)

Again, we see her immediately afterwards in the act of pleasing and it tells us how easily Sir Walter can be pleased, as well as how ironically the narrator views her skills. She is trying to suggest that all professional men lose their looks quickly and that only idle land-owners can keep them:

> 'The lawyer plods, quite care-worn; the physician is up at all hours, and travelling in all weather; and even the clergyman—' she stopt a moment to consider what might do for the clergyman;—'and even the clergyman, you know, is obliged to go into infected rooms.' (Chapter 3)

(iii) Both Lady Russell and Mrs Clay have parallels in the plot of the novel; these parallels help the reader to define and understand the issues just as the parallel between Mr Elliot and Captain Wentworth does. Lady Russell is compared unfavourably with Mrs Musgrove; in Chapter 14 Mr and Mrs Musgrove are the centre of 'a fine family-piece' at Christmas but Lady Russell says she will never visit them again at Christmas because of the noise though she enjoys 'the heavy rumble of carts and drays, the bawling of newsmen . . . and the ceaseless clink of pattens' in Bath. As Lady Russell is *in loco parentis* (in the place of a parent) to Anne we compare her attitude to Anne's engagement with Mrs Musgrove's to Henrietta's: 'Though we could have wished it different . . . we thought they had better marry at once, and make the best of it, as many others have done before them' (Chapter 23). Similarly Mrs Clay is compared with Mrs Smith: 'Mrs Smith was not the only widow in Bath between thirty and forty, with little to live on, and no sirname of dignity' (Chapter 17).

(*iv*) Both Lady Russell and Mrs Clay are members of Sir Walter's group and both are powerfully persuasive. Henrietta says of Lady Russell: 'I always look upon her as able to persuade a person to anything!' (Chapter 12) At the end of the novel Mrs Clay has become Mr Elliot's mistress and 'it is now a doubtful point whether his cunning, or hers, may finally carry the day; whether, after preventing her from being the wife of Sir Walter, he may not be wheedled and caressed at last into making her the wife of Sir William' (Chapter 24). Both contribute towards the meaning of the title. The book is about the interaction of people in society and their ability to influence each other's actions: Lady Russell almost persuades Anne to think of marrying Mr Elliot. She is made to 'shudder at the idea of the misery which must have followed. It was just possible that she might have been persuaded by Lady Russell!' (Chapter 21). Similarly Mrs Clay exerts her influence over Sir Walter and Elizabeth.

(*v*) As members of Sir Walter's group Lady Russell and Mrs Clay both have the limitations of snobbery. Lady Russell encourages the Dalrymple connection: 'Family connexions were always worth preserving, good company always worth seeking; Lady Dalrymple . . . would be living in style' (Chapter 16). Eventually this snobbery seriously compromises Lady Russell's famous integrity; she accepts Mr Elliot because he is an Elliot, just as she disapproved of Captain Wentworth because he had no fortune or rank.

(*vi*) Both Lady Russell and Mrs Clay serve as a foil for Anne. Elizabeth prefers Mrs Clay as a confidante and friend, 'turning from the society of so deserving a sister to bestow her affection and confidence on one who ought to have been nothing to her but the object of distant civility' (Chapter 2). The reader measures Anne's insight by the comparison the narrator makes between her and Lady Russell; Lady Russell is renowned for her rectitude but Anne compares favourably with her: 'there is a quickness of perception in some, a nicety in the discernment of character, a natural penetration, in short, which no experience in others can equal, and Lady Russell had been less gifted in this part of understanding than her young friend' (Chapter 24).

Suggested outline of answer to (3)

Many of the points used in the sample answer to Question (1) would also apply here. The essay should establish first how difficult it is to attain successfully realistic presentation. It could then centre on the depiction of Anne, by showing how the reader sees through Anne's eyes and does not know what Captain Wentworth thinks. As a result he scrutinises Captain Wentworth's behaviour as Anne does, and is almost as aware as she is of favourable omens.

Part 5

Suggestions for further reading

The text

Persuasion, edited by R.W. Chapman, published with *Northanger Abbey* and a *Biographical Notice* of the Author by Henry Austen, in Vol. V of *The Novels of Jane Austen*, Clarendon Press, Oxford, 1923
Persuasion with *A Memoir of Jane Austen* by J.E. Austen-Leigh, edited by D.W. Harding, Penguin Books, Harmondsworth, 1965

Other novels by Jane Austen

Sense and Sensibility, first published in 1811
Pride and Prejudice, first published in 1813
Mansfield Park, first published in 1814
Emma, first published in 1816
Northanger Abbey, first published with *Persuasion* in 1818

Other works by Jane Austen

Jane Austen's juvenilia and fragments of novels are collected and published as *The Works of Jane Austen: Volume VI, Minor Works*, edited by R.W. Chapman, Oxford University Press, London, 1954
Jane Austen's Letters collected and edited by R.W. Chapman 2nd edition, Oxford University Press, London, 1952

General reading

CHAPMAN, R.W.: *Jane Austen: Facts and Problems*, Oxford University Press, London, 1948
SOUTHAM, B.C.: *Jane Austen's Literary Manuscripts*, Clarendon Press, Oxford, 1964

Both these books contain scholarly information useful for the study of Jane Austen's life and works.
The following are useful critical studies of Jane Austen's fiction:

DUCKWORTH, ALISTAIR M.: *The Improvement of the Estate: a Study of Jane Austen's Novels*, Johns Hopkins Press, Baltimore and London, 1971

LASCELLES, MARY: *Jane Austen and her Art*, Oxford University Press, London, 1939

MUDRICK, MARVIN: *Jane Austen: Irony as Defense and Discovery*, Oxford University Press, London, 1952

WRIGHT, ANDREW H.: *Jane Austen's Novels: a Study in Structure*, Chatto and Windus, London, 1953

HARDING, D.W.: 'Regulated Hatred: an Aspect of the Work of Jane Austen', *Scrutiny* VIII, 1940, pp.346-62

The author of these notes

ANGELA SMITH read English at the Universities of Birmingham and Cambridge. She has taught in Los Angeles and Wales and is now a lecturer in English Studies at the University of Stirling, where she has special responsibilities in the teaching of Commonwealth Literature. She has also worked part-time for the Open University since its inception.